Those are fools however learned who have
not learned to walk with the world.

Thiruvalluvar

Kanyakumari

HAZEL MANUEL

CinnamonPress

INDEPENDENT INNOVATIVE INTERNATIONAL

Published by Cinnamon Press,
Meirion House,
Tanygrisiau,
Blaenau Ffestiniog,
Gwynedd
LL41 3SU
www.cinnamonpress.com

ISBN 978-1-909077-27-0
British Library Cataloguing in Publication Data. A CIP record for
this book can be obtained from the British Library.

Cinnamon Press is represented by Inpress and by the Welsh Books
Council in Wales.

Printed in Poland

The publisher acknowledges the support of the Welsh Books
Council

Prologue

The beach is quiet. White robes flutter and bare feet bury themselves in soft, damp sand. The faintest of breezes ruffles cloth and hair, warm and sweet as it mingles with incense smoke. Aromas of cinnamon, cardamom and sandalwood perfume the air and drift along the deserted shore.

They kneel together close to the water's edge. The sea, as restless as fire, is waiting to consume the red sun as it sinks into the dark water. Two women hold hands. Their fingers grasp one another's tightly as they kneel on the sand. Another woman kneels beside them, holding a paper lamp in her lap, knotted blue veins on the backs on her bony hands, maps of complex history written into her body. A little wax candle at the centre of the lamp burns, its flame dancing in the paper holder as the breeze whispers around it. A necklace of small wooden beads is wound around the base of the lamp, and jasmine and rose petals have been placed around the beads. A single shell sits on the lamp.

Still holding hands, they watch as the older woman stands, steadying herself a little as she rises, before taking a step towards the water's edge. The flame burns as she stands still for a moment, gazing ahead of her, beyond the horizon. The water caresses her feet, warm as blood, as the hem of her robe becomes wet and sticks to her ankles. She holds the lamp out in front of her and murmurs. The words are intoned quietly, offered up to the waiting sea, which accepts them and gives them to the breeze.

'O, Supreme light, lead us from untruth to truth, from darkness to light and from death to immortality.'

She stoops slightly to place the lamp gently in the water. She gives it a little push before standing to chant once more:

'The wheel of life moves on. Youth, beauty, life, possessions, health and the companionship of friends, all are unstable. Our life on this earth comes to an end, but the soul journeys on. The soul is immortal. The soul is not born and shall never die.'

They watch in silence as the lamp bobs, its flame flickering gently, a scattering of white petals dropping into the darkening water. She stands for a while. The sea is taking the sun, and streaks of red, orange and purple pour into the sky and across the water. An almost imperceptible sigh follows her gaze. She drops her eyes, closes them momentarily, turns away and returns to kneel on the sand.

The women watch as the lamp rises and falls, its jerky movements brave in the face of the vast crimson ocean, as the water carries it further from the shore. Each woman feels the rising certainty of a resolution, of an ending and a beginning. She closes her eyes as her intonation comes, resonant and low:

'Life is a river which starts at the source and ends at the ocean. Saraswati surpasses all other rivers to flow pure from the mountains to the sea. She descends from the great mountain to the sacrifice. May the universal mother bless us with wisdom, peace and immortal bliss. May we, with her grace and blessing, be absolutely free.'

The sun casts its red death towards the women. It reaches for the lamp and very soon the flame is gone. The sea accepts the offering of beads and they are borne away to the depths beneath the surface. The shell is all that is left now. It floats there on the lamp for a moment, fragile and pure, before disappearing below the surface as the sun breathes its final breath and is taken by the sea.

'*Om Asato Ma sad gamaya, Om Tamaso ma jyotirgamaya, Om Mrityorma amritam gamaya. Om Shanti, Shanti, Shanti.*'

Chapter 1 – Rachel

'Bribery? Seriously?'

Rachel added it to the list of experiences she had accumulated in her thirty-one years. It made her smile because it made her feel daring, standing there with Pravi in the confined space of the ticket office, the slow and creaking overhead fan trying half-heartedly to stir the fetid air.

Pravi cocked an eyebrow. 'The problem is, Rachel, since we've left buying the tickets until now, there won't be enough places left.'

Such is the price of spontaneity, thought Rachel as she wiped an irritating trickle of sweat from the side of her face.

'Rachel, do not concern yourself with this,' Pravi whispered to her. She felt his hot breath, his lips almost touching her ear. 'We will get our tickets. This is the way of it in India.'

As they waited, a short young man dressed in jeans and an oversized orange tee-shirt slid furtively beside them and mumbled something barely audible to Pravi. She couldn't catch what language he was speaking in, probably Tamil, she thought. The man stank of sweat and didn't make eye contact with anyone. Pravi mumbled something back to him, took out his wallet surreptitiously and slipped him some rupees. The man backed into the crowd and sidled away.

Rachel watched, fascinated, as the grubby notes changed hands. 'This is amazing,' she said. 'I thought we weren't going to be able to go. Is it normal to buy a ticket like this?'

Pravi didn't answer and Rachel continued to watch, fascinated, as the man left the ticket office, came back some moments later and started to work his way slowly closer to the scratched wooden counter with a crowd of grimy and weary-looking men.

'Seriously, Pravi,' Rachel whispered into his ear, 'Are you used to this way of getting things done?'

Pravi simply laughed.

Rachel didn't remember what she had expected when she and Gina decided that they would visit India. Some vague notion of temples and elephants and spicy food probably. It wasn't that she was naive; she had expected to see the poverty and the beggars. 'We'll just have to be hardened to it,' she had said to Gina. But the complex interplay of poverty, bureaucracy and corruption had of course evaded her when sitting with her friend in Gina's living room, flicking through her *Lonely Planet* guide, gazing at pictures of pretty women in colourful saris, serious-looking holy men and aerial shots of fields full of strange-looking, brightly coloured crops.

Now, in the rank and grimy ticket office, those with the means to do so were able to jump the queue, thanks to the discreet black-marketeers. There she stood with Pravi in Kanyakumari station amid the murmuring and the shuffling, pushed up against a mass of dark-skinned men, all of them sweating profusely, all grimly intent on getting to the ticket counter. The fact that there was no queue appeared not to matter. Neither did it seem to matter that everyone was pushing and shoving in swaying slow motion which held no suggestion of aggression but only resignation and the lethargic belief that each man would reach the ticket counter sooner or later. Rachel looked around and wondered if all these people were hoping to travel or whether some were there just to do the bribing. She realised that their bribe would probably mean that some of those without the necessary means wouldn't get tickets. She looked around at the brown faces and saw that no one was smiling.

The rank smell of hot bodies was overwhelming and everyone waiting in the ticket office looked poor. She wondered where they were hoping to travel. Pravi pointed out a group of people who he said were from elsewhere. He could tell, he said, because their features were different from those of natives of the south – they had thinner noses and sharper cheekbones.

'They come here for work,' Pravi said. 'There is more seasonal employment on the coast, in the hotels and with tourist activities. These men are probably going back north to spend time with their families.'

Rachel suppressed another spike of guilt. After all, she said to herself, this is the way things are done here.

The heat in the small and densely crowded room felt dirty and oppressive. Rachel was exhausted although it was still only mid-morning. She looked at the pitiful fan with scorn as it squeaked and wobbled and did nothing to alleviate the damp stickiness that made her shirt stick to her back and the sweat itch on her forehead. She wiped her brow on the arm of her shirt, noting with annoyance the dirty sweat-mark left on her sleeve. She could feel her hair clinging in clumps around her face, pushed it back with irritation and re-tied it into a tighter ponytail, trying not to elbow the men around her. She was astounded at how tiring and time-consuming it was simply to buy a train ticket, and she wondered in exasperation how anything ever got done here.

'Pravi, he's at the ticket desk now,' she said quietly. She couldn't see what was happening, but Pravi had whispered to her that money would have changed hands when the man left the ticket office and the tickets would now be waiting.

'The man is probably related to one of the railway officials,' Pravi said. 'He paid him a cut when he went outside.' He wouldn't have handed over as much money as Pravi had given him, of course. The bribe-man had to take his cut. Rachel supposed that this was his job of sorts. She wondered whether he had a family, a mother and father, siblings who were dependent on his income. She wondered about the railway official who had accepted his bribe. She thought uncomfortably of the thousands, probably millions, of small, black-market transactions that enabled so many of the people of this country to go about their daily lives, but stopped others going about theirs. But this is India, Rachel reasoned to herself. It runs according to its own rules.

The bribe-man turned from the ticket counter, nodded almost imperceptibly at Pravi making the briefest of eye contact before sidling once more into the crowd. Rachel and Pravi pushed their way to the door to meet him outside. Minutes later, they were standing by the station entrance, squinting in the glaring midday sun, sweating and smiling and clutching two second-class air-conditioned tickets to Mumbai.

Chapter 2 – Gina

Bitch! Gina stared at the empty bed beside hers through narrowed eyes. She'd woken up late feeling muzzy and groped immediately for her cigarettes, fumbling amongst the debris on her bedside table. She rolled onto her side and lit one, flicking the lighter impatiently two or three times before it caught, and took a deep drag, half lying, half sitting, propped on one elbow. She closed her eyes as she felt the remaining miasma of sleep retreating. She'd had the dream again. Its tendrils still caught at the edges of her mind, and she took another deep drag of her cigarette, willing its memory to disperse with the smoke. She thought about telling Rachel about it this time. She took another long drag on her cigarette, opened her eyes, and turned towards Rachel's bed. The jolt of anger she felt jerked her fully awake. Of course, Rachel had gone to Mumbai with Pravi. She hadn't even bothered to say goodbye. 'Damned woman,' she muttered as she rubbed her hand absently across her abdomen and stared up at the ceiling taking deep drags of her cigarette.

After some minutes Gina swung her legs out of bed and stretched. She ground her spent cigarette into the ashtray and made her way to the kitchen with a glance at her watch. She supposed Rachel would be on the train by now and felt another wave of resentment. In the tiny kitchen she took another cigarette from a pack she found by the sink before half filling the kettle with bottled water from the enormous and ancient fridge. 'Damned thing,' she muttered as she looked around for a lighter before making coffee. Yawning widely, she walked through to the anteroom and opened the French doors, almost dropping her coffee as she struggled with it and her cigarette and lighter and the door handle.

The heat smacked her in the face, making Gina think of Thailand as she confronted it and stepped onto the balcony. The tiles were hot under her bare feet, and Gina put her coffee cup down on the floor and went back inside to get an ashtray and her flip-flops. She caught sight of a bottle of sun cream on the nightstand and picked that up as well. Once settled, she looked down at the path. No one was there. She opened the bottle of sun cream and smoothed the lotion into her arms and legs, face and neck.

Gina suddenly thought that, since Rachel had left early, she might not have wanted to wake her and had perhaps left her a message instead of saying goodbye. There was no note in any obvious place in the anteroom or in the kitchen. She walked through the bedroom, thinking that perhaps Rachel had left it on her bed. The bed was unmade and there was no note there either. Gina's fury returned, a savage thing, and she bit down hard on it until her lip bled.

Last time they had travelled it had been to Thailand, and they'd spent weeks planning and preparing, obtaining the visas, making sure their vaccinations were up to date, reading about the surrounding area, its wildlife, its people, thinking up possible itineraries and finally deciding on their route, booking the accommodation, contacting people who had been, getting contact details of friends of friends who might be there when they were. And the trip had been a success: travelling, making friends, sightseeing and relaxing by the ocean. But it hadn't been like that with this trip.

Gina yawned and told herself that she should think about the day ahead, plan to do something with her time. Was it four or five days Rachel would be away? She couldn't remember the exact details. The time seemed to stretch ahead of her like a challenge. She had been keen to go to a tiger sanctuary that she had read about on the internet. It was a couple of hours away from their hotel, and they had tried to book an organised trip to it a few days ago, but had left it too late. At the time, Gina had been annoyed and blamed Rachel, but had decided that perhaps that wasn't really fair. Now she wasn't so sure. But in any case, she thought, the sanctuary would make a good trip, if not today then tomorrow; she supposed that she could plan to get there independently by bus or even taxi. Gina sipped her coffee and was considering this when the beeping of her mobile made her jump – a text message. Instantly cheered – the message would surely be from Rachel – she put her coffee down and went inside. After hunting for her phone, she found it attached to its charger amongst a pile of clothes by her bed and was pleased to see that the message was indeed from Rachel. It was not much of a message though, Gina thought with a new spike of irritation. 'I'm off to Mumbai, have a good few days.' There wasn't even anything to say exactly when Rachel would be back. Damned typical, thought Gina, but nonetheless she texted back saying that she hoped Rachel would have a good time. She sighed and flung the phone onto her bed. There was nothing to be gained, she thought, from being mean-spirited, and although she felt let down by Rachel, the best way forward, she decided, was to get on with her own plans as soon as she decided what they were.

But even so, as Gina settled herself back on the balcony with her coffee and picked up the cigarette that was burning away in the ashtray, she couldn't deny her feelings of resentment. Gina's expectation had been that they would decide together what to do with their time. She certainly didn't want to be by herself. She looked over the balcony and wondered why the place seemed so deserted, as though everyone else in the world had somewhere to be and someone to be there with. It must be breakfast time, she thought. She wasn't hungry. She wondered, not for the first time, if she should have spoken to Rachel before she left, talked to her about what had happened. Her dream pushed itself into her mind, and Gina closed her eyes and fought to suppress it. She re-lit her cigarette and sipped her cooling coffee, trying to focus on the trip to the tiger sanctuary.

But her thoughts returned to Rachel. What hurt her was not simply that she had gone to Mumbai, but that she had gone with someone else, someone they had met only a week ago. She thought about Pravi. He seemed likeable, and he had a quiet wit that Gina appreciated. But she was rather more cynical about him than Rachel, and it seemed incredible to her that Rachel would go off with a man she hardly knew. Gina frowned and pursed her lips. After all, what did they really know about Pravi beyond the fact that he was an attractive young musician?

Chapter 3 – Sandrine

15th July 1967

My dear Perelle,

So, here I am, my darling brother, in India. I am in Varanassi, which I am sure you know is the Hindu holy city on the banks of the mighty and sacred River Ganges. Mother Ganga, as it is called here. I have a little while before my train to Lucknow arrives, and so I thought I would use the time to send you a letter from this holy place – it seems fitting. I was pleased to receive your letter. It was waiting for me at the hotel when I arrived. Thank you for your kind words about my voyage here and my journey to Varanassi. But really, Perelle, tell Papa not to fuss. I will be here for some time to come, and he really must get used to this simple fact. Tell him also that my allowance was waiting for me and I had no problem accessing it. I am as grateful for his financial support as I am for your emotional support, on which I am sure I can count.

Perelle, I have witnessed things here that I can barely describe, and my meagre words will certainly fail to convey to you all that I have felt and seen and done. I have seen dead bodies being burned on the Ghats, the sunset Arti ceremony at the edge of Ganges (thousands of people were there – more than I have ever seen in one place at home in Paris!), and I have been blessed by a yogi. I have visited temples and have seen such desperate, aching poverty in people with open, smiling faces who would share their last morsel with you. Nothing is as one would expect it to be here. Half-naked little children somewhat disconcertingly run up to you and ask if you want to "see dead body burning"! It is because that is the way they cremate their dead, Perelle, right there in the open on a pile of wood beside the sacred river. And when the body is burned the ashes go into the river, back to the mother as they refer to it. The child to whom I refer took me there to the funeral ghat where a man was being cremated. I could see his face clearly, smell the acrid scent of his flesh burning, and I stood for a long time and watched as the flames gradually consumed the wood beneath and around him. Lying amid the smoke and the flames, the dead man looked strangely serene, as though in death he had finally found a way to sleep deeply, and I felt something akin to envy. I thought I would have felt more, watching a human body burn, but mostly I simply felt a detached sort of curiosity. There are other things here that move me more than the destruction of an empty body.

I am finding that, if one can look past the squalor and the beggars and the stench of human bodies and rubbish, there is something wondrous here, something that adheres in the people, in the land, in the very air itself. I love seeing the bright saris and smelling the incense wafting around the temples. I love seeing the wide open smiles on the faces of wretched little street children. I visited some people in a tiny village the other day, and the women were fascinated with my eyes – I think because they are blue and they probably hadn't seen many people with blue eyes. The women were also interested in my clothes, which they weren't shy about examining in minute detail. One gave me her tiny baby to hold, he was adorable, all big brown eyes and gurgling laughter – I think it is easy to make friends with women if one can get to meet them because there are lots of points of contact that don't require language. They gave me some water to drink, which was awkward because I didn't know if it had been boiled. I had to sip it though as I was sitting with the ladies and the children and didn't want to appear rude.

Perelle, I'm off now to get things for the train journey to Lucknow – it is a long overnight journey so, my darling brother, I will write more in a few days. Give my regards to Papa and tell him not to worry – my tour has begun well and I am happy and safe. You have the address for post in Lucknow, so I will await your letter there.

Chapter 4 – Rachel

'Gina, I don't know why you won't come. We did say we'd go to Mumbai when we were planning the trip.'

They had been at a bar close to their hotel, and Pravi was getting drinks. His friend Ajit looked from one to the other as he knocked back the last of his beer and set the bottle down in front of him.

Gina looked at Ajit and quickly back at Rachel. 'The journey will take too long. It will be too tiring. I just want to chill out,' she said.

Rachel looked at her with a slight frown. 'Oh Gina, you should come,' she said, trying to keep her impatience out of her voice. 'You know you'll enjoy it once we're on our way. You always love an exciting trip.'

'Look Rachel, I'm not being funny, but I told you the other day when you first planned this that I'm not going. Can we just leave it now?'

Pravi returned, balancing four bottles of beer in his hands. 'Everything okay?' he said, looking at Rachel as he set the bottles down on the table.

'It looks like you and Rachel are going to Mumbai on your own, my friend,' Ajit said, grabbing a bottle and clinking it against Pravi's.

Rachel had woken on the morning of her trip with a tight knot of excitement in her stomach, which made her impatient to leave. Pravi was waiting in the car park, and Rachel looked at him leaning against his motorbike, the bright sun glinting off his sunglasses, one leg cocked, a foot resting on a pedal, his jeans stretched tight across his thighs. Rachel smiled quickly and looked away. They rode the half an hour into town, and although it wasn't the first time Rachel had been on the back of Pravi's bike, it nonetheless thrilled her to be speeding along past the hotels and shacks and onto the open road, her hair streaming behind her in the wind. Rachel was pleased to get away from the tourist area. She liked to think of herself as a traveller rather than a tourist. The distinction was important to her, and being with Pravi made her feel more connected to the place. On the back of the bike she could feel Pravi's heat against her thighs, and a snatch of an old song flew into her mind and out again and made her grin widely. Something about a woman who would never ride in a sports car through Paris. This, she thought, is my sports car; this is my Paris. She tried to lock herself into the moment, to feel as much of her freedom as she could.

They stopped at the bridge and Pravi got off the bike to put on his helmet. Rachel laughed out loud at this.

'We can ride without helmets anywhere but not on the bridge,' Pravi told her as he shook out his thick dark hair. 'If we don't wear them, the police may stop us and detain us until we pay a suitable bribe.'

'Seriously?' Rachel said and laughed to find out that only the driver had to wear a helmet. Passengers were free to cross the bridge bareheaded.

Once over the bridge they stopped once more and Pravi took off his helmet. Rachel smiled. It somehow seemed to underline all that was different, unfathomable, wonderfully mystifying about this place.

When they arrived at the outskirts of the town, Pravi took his bike to a friend's shop and left it there. 'It will be much safer to leave it here whilst we are away,' he told Rachel. He and his friend clasped one another's shoulders, talked a lot in Tamil, laughed together. The friend looked at Rachel and smiled broadly, and Rachel wondered but didn't ask what Pravi had said to him. She smiled back and cocked an eyebrow at Pravi, who raised both of his eyebrows and his shoulders at her in mock innocence. They then walked the short distance along a pot-holed street to the bus station. Rachel stood in the heat and the heave of the place as people swarmed all around her, and she watched in amazement and awe as men stood outside the buses and shouted their destinations at the tops of their voices and at a speed which rendered their words almost incomprehensible. A bony cow lumbered in a leisurely way through the crowd. Pravi led her towards a gaily painted bus, decked out with strings of wooden beads and garlands of orange flowers, where a man in a grey shirt and white lungi was shouting 'CormorinCormorinCormorin' and ignoring everyone. Rachel tried saying 'Cormorin' in her head over and over again fast, but couldn't articulate the words the way the bus man could. She supposed it must take practice. The thought of the bus men practising their destinations made her laugh.

Pravi explained as they climbed onto the bus that it wouldn't leave until it was full.

'Isn't that a problem for people who have to be somewhere at a certain time – like a station?' she asked.

'The answer, Rachel,' Pravi said, smiling at her, 'is simply to leave plenty of time to allow for this.'

It appeared to her that everything in this country happened both frenetically and interminably slowly. She sat and watched as the bus gradually filled with an array of colourfully dressed women, skinny children and men of all ages, some wearing kurtas or Punjabi pyjamas, some in western-style trousers and short-sleeved shirts. Each took their place, the younger ones talking and laughing, the older ones in sombre silence, and when all the seats were taken more got on and stood, holding onto the backs of the chairs, becoming steadily more pressed as the bus reached capacity. Some little boys in grey shorts sat on the floor and stared up at Rachel with honest eyes, whispering and giggling to one another. Rachel smiled and wished she had some sweets to give them. Only when no more passengers could possibly fit into the bus did it eventually start up and set off, amid much shuddering and growling of the ancient engine. Eyes turned to the windows, and Rachel joined the other passengers in staring at the world outside as though it were some remarkable place which required study and analysis. Which, as far as Rachel was concerned, it did.

Rachel recognised the route they took, as she and Gina had been into Kanyakumari together during their first week here, and she watched as the bus hurtled at an unlikely and somewhat unnerving speed past the Hindu temples, shops and shacks. She thought back to the temple they had visited, the Kumari Amman, with its great towering shrines and grimacing statues. She had stood for a long time in front of Shree Bhagavarthy, breathing in the sweet smell of insense, inexplicably feeling tears behind her eyes. 'She is the goddess of penance' a Pandit had said to her. She turned around. He was demure and self effacing in his long green lungi and had offered to show them where the ceremonial cart and other religious artifacts were stored. The cart was huge and ornately carved. Its wooden wheels were taller than she was, and Rachel had felt dwarfed, both physically and spiritually, by its solid and powerful presence. She thought of it rolling slowly through the town, decked out in bright garlands, incense burning, colourfully dressed men and women following and little children running alongside it joyfully. It had made her feel somehow left out, lonely even, because she didn't understand the significance, the meaning of it and she vowed to herself to buy a book about the Hindu religion when she returned home. 'Madam, you will very soon meet a rich man,' the Pandit had said to her outside the cart store. She had laughed and told him that she wasn't particularly drawn to men with money. The Pandit had replied seriously and enigmatically, '"rich" can mean many things.'

Pravi patted Rachel's shoulder as the bus shuddered to a stop, and she felt a jolt of wellbeing, warm and strong, as they stood and gathered their backpacks from beneath the seat in front of them. She suppressed a giggle as she glanced at Pravi, who was struggling to retrieve his pack and whose big, wild curls were bouncing around his head as though he had received an electric shock.

Once off the bus, Pravi had suggested that they buy some food for the journey, and they headed off to a nearby collection of stalls where old men were selling melons, dates, mangoes and apples. 'There will of course be food on the train, but we should buy extra,' Pravi said, as he squeezed a mango.

They bought apples and peanuts, agreeing with one another that these would survive the journey better than the softer fruit. While Rachel was stuffing the apples into her backpack, Pravi waved and called out to a young man on a scooter and jogged over to him. Rachel watched as Pravi wobbled his head as he greeted the man and then walked over as he waved to her.

'Very fortuitous!' Pravi exclaimed brightly. 'Kaimal has offered us a lift to the station on his bike.'

Rachel looked doubtfully at the scooter and the man and wondered how three people and two backpacks could fit on this thing. But as they rode through the busy streets, Rachel clinging to the back as best she could, she smiled to herself. *India*, she thought, as they swerved past a slumbering cow.

Chapter 5 – Gina

Gina stepped gingerly out of the shower and reached for one of the big white hotel towels that she had folded and placed onto the toilet seat. It felt warm and soft as she wrapped herself in it, and she closed her eyes and savoured the cosy feel of the soft material against her damp skin. She sighed as she pulled the towel tightly around her, tucking the loose end into the top securely. But the little ritual failed to comfort her as it usually did, and Gina thought fleetingly of Rachel, wondering where she was in her journey. The small bathroom was full of steam and Gina wiped the mirror above the basin with her hand, leaving a brightly shiny, curved smear which quickly disappeared as the mirror steamed up again, making her face appear ghostly and ethereal. She picked up her toothbrush and looked at it. It somehow looked redundant and Gina felt as though she had to force herself to pick up the toothpaste, unscrew the top and squeeze some paste onto the brush. She almost couldn't be bothered; it was too hot and she vaguely intended to go for a swim anyhow, making all this effort in the bathroom seem futile, but she had quickly told herself that she was being silly; she had to look after herself. She smiled wanly at this as she set resolutely about cleaning her teeth, telling herself that she wasn't the kind of person to crumble just because she was to be on her own in a foreign country for a few days. 'Damned ridiculous,' she said out loud to her ghostly mirror-self.

Gina opened the bathroom door to let out the steam and set about towelling her hair. She tipped her head upside down in front of her and rubbed her head vigorously with a hand towel, feeling somehow more in control for having made the effort. It was a good start, she told herself; she was getting ready for the day ahead. The days ahead. The time seemed to slide away from her, and Gina wondered what she would do with herself. But, no matter, she thought, the first thing is to get ready. She could then have a coffee, perhaps something to eat in the restaurant, and then she could plan her day. One thing at a time. Gina prided herself on her practicality. 'Such a clever, sensible girl,' her mother had always said. 'You'll always be okay with that practical nature of yours.' It was, Gina considered, her 'thing', and over the years positive reinforcement of this quality had encouraged her to hone it, to refine it into a sleek and seemingly effortless ability to simply 'cope'. Her boss at the publishing house where she worked had remarked encouragingly in her last appraisal on her commonsense and her ability to deal with difficulties in a level-headed and balanced way. 'You, Gina, are what popular group-dynamics theory calls a 'problem-solver,' he had told her. Her practicality was enhanced by the fact that Gina considered emotional responses to be unhelpful in most situations and actively tried to apply this to her work and to her life. This tended to give her an air of poised self-assurance and had stood her in good stead at work, where her consistency and unflappable approach had been noted. 'I'll tell you what, Mike,' Gina had once overheard her boss saying to a colleague, 'she might be what you'd call a bit of a cold fish, but the one person I know I can rely on in a crisis is Gina.' Gina sometimes wondered, though, if she appeared too cold at times, and she had been told by the same boss that some people found her focus and her

26

organisational skills rather intimidating. But now, here, on her own, she certainly didn't feel as though she could intimidate anyone. 'One thing at a time,' she repeated firmly to herself.

She tied her hair up into the towel, turban-style, and turned back to the mirror. The steam had retreated, and Gina leant her hands on the basin in front of her, stretched out her arms and stared at herself in the glass. She stood like that for some time, looking intently at her face, her eyes, her lips, her skin. 'This,' she thought, 'is me. Practical, sensible, organised Gina.' The idea suddenly seemed miraculous. She tried to work out what the words meant, what their connection was with the face that gazed back at her steadily from the glass. The brown eyes stared out at her, round and blank, and she stared back. Was there life in them? The more she stared, the more disengaged she felt, until the thing in the mirror ceased to be her face at all, mutating into a disembodied collection of colours and shapes which hovered pink and fleshy before her. Suddenly alarmed, she swayed and clutched the sink, bent her head and heaved into it but didn't actually vomit. She closed her eyes and took a deep breath. 'I need a cigarette' she muttered as she turned to leave the room.

Chapter 6 – Sandrine

27th July 1967

Darling Perelle,
I hoped for a letter from you, but it was not to be. Perhaps I left my last place too soon and missed it. My darling brother, do write to me whenever you can, you must know how very much I miss you. My last train ride was very difficult indeed; long, hot, uncomfortable, tiring. A man was in my seat by the window and he wouldn't move. My seat was so hard that I couldn't sleep and was exhausted all the way, in that state where one feels sick and ill, one is so tired. But I am in Agra now and the Taj Mahal is just wonderful – bigger and more majestic than ever I imagined. Agra is a sprawling town, loud, dirty, busy and crowded. Its centre is alive with carts, cows, rickshaws, barefoot running children, and all manner of humanity going about their daily life. I feel outside it all here Perelle. It isn't the dirt and the poverty that repel me, those things are surface and there is enough beauty here that the squalor can be looked through. No, what I don't like is the fact of my own difference here, my lack of insight. I wonder whether this will ever change?

The man was there to meet me at Agra station, and he took me to the house, which is lovely – basic but spotlessly clean. The lady and the man are really very kind. There was food waiting for me, potatoes and onions cooked in yogurt, cumin, coriander, cardamom, cinnamon, turmeric and ground chilies and although they speak almost no English (and of course no French) they really made me feel most welcome through their gestures and smiles, which reach all the way up from their mouths to their eyes. I woke at about six o'clock this morning, Perelle, and I thought I might as well get up. The couple were already up – it appears that Indians generally rise very early as it is cool then and light. I went for a long walk this morning by myself, and I kept walking south as I didn't want to get lost in the town. I found myself in some cucumber fields with lots of men and women and even children working in them. A lady offered me some cucumbers, but I said no thank you. I wish I had accepted now. At lunchtime the lady (whom we have to call Amma, which means mother) had made rice and aubergines cooked with garlic, ginger, mustard seeds and cumin. Perelle, the food here is divine! And in the afternoon I took a rickshaw into the town centre, which turned out to be not so bad at all. I walked, talking to random people, which they liked, although of course no one understood me, and then I went to buy some fruit – I bought two mangoes which were soft and orange and smelt just wonderful. After that, I came back and drank gallons of water and went to lie down until now, when I have decided to write to you, my love. I am missing you very much indeed, Perelle, but I am relieved that things are going well. Tomorrow I am being taken to visit the palace of Fatehpur Sikri and beyond that I will think about leaving. I want to hear news about your lectureship. I am so proud of my clever brother and wish to hear how your new post is for you. You must work hard and not waste this opportunity. I am sure that Papa has told you the same. Anyway, dear Perelle, I'm going to end now. I love you, darling brother, and I miss you, but am so happy that you are supportive of this silly mission of mine.

Chapter 7 – Rachel

The train was late and the sun was callous as they waited at the far end of the station, where the stationmaster had directed them. Pravi had bought a lassi from a station vendor and shared it with Rachel. As they sweated profusely in the morning heat, they were both glad that they had brought plenty of bottled water with them. Rachel took hers out and drank deeply from the warm plastic bottle, offering it to Pravi who gladly accepted it. Rachel was intrigued that he didn't put the bottle to his lips but instead threw his head back and tipped the water into his open mouth. She had read somewhere that people of a particular religion did this – was it Hindus or Muslims? Or maybe both, she thought, turning to look up and down the surprisingly uncrowded platforms.

'You know, I love stations,' she told Pravi. 'I love the feeling that I'm on my way to somewhere. It makes me feel as though, whatever life is, it can still be more.'

Pravi smiled at her.

Rachel stared along the empty railway line and into the waiting horizon. Somewhere along that track Mumbai is waiting for me, she thought. She smiled broadly at Pravi, who was also staring up the track, his hair dancing in dark, wild curls around his face.

The trip had been planned by text message. 'I hv a crzy idea,' Rachel had texted. 'Cm 2 MBai wth me.' And Pravi had texted back, 'Ok I'll cm.' Rachel had felt a surge of excitement in her stomach. She had re-read it and smiled. She hadn't been sure when she sent the text to Pravi whether her suggestion was actually serious, and she didn't know how Pravi would respond. But his reply sealed the plan. Rachel hadn't told Gina when the text came. Instead she told her later on, over lunch.

'Gina,' she said, 'Are you certain you won't come to Mumbai?'

'Rachel please, don't keep talking about Mumbai. I've made it clear I don't want to go, I'm really sorry but I just don't.' Gina's voice was impatient as though she were talking to an annoying child.

'I understand that,' Rachel replied, 'but you know how much I was looking forward to going?' Gina opened her mouth to respond, but Rachel spoke quickly. 'What would you think if I went?' Her voice was quiet.

'What, on your own?' Gina was dismissive. 'That doesn't sound like a good idea at all.'

'No, not on my own,' Rachel said. 'With Pravi.'

'With Pravi?' Gina exclaimed, her eyes widening. A song from an Indian film was playing in the background, and the other people at the restaurant were laughing and talking. Gina stared at Rachel.

'Yes, with Pravi. I've asked him, and he says that he's willing to go with me.'

'You've asked him already?'

'Yes. We're going into Kanyakumari soon to get the tickets.'

Gina finished her drink, setting the glass carefully on the cane table in front of her. She leaned back in her seat, still staring at Rachel. A man caught her shoulder with his jacket as he passed and apologised. Gina ignored him.

'Well,' she said quietly, 'if that's what you want to do.'

The next day had dawned hot and bright, and Rachel and Gina had spent the morning hunting for bargains in the shacks by the beach. They didn't speak about Rachel's trip to Mumbai again until the evening when they were sipping juice at a beach-front shack they had walked to along the beach. It took them most of the afternoon, and they had to stop a few times to buy water to help them to cope with the searing heat of the sun. As they walked, they talked about what they might do that evening.

'I don't think I'll need to eat much tonight. Will you?' Rachel asked.

'No, this heat just makes me need to drink gallons,' Gina replied. 'Shall we go to the juice bar?'

They sat on the quiet wooden balcony overlooking the restless sea, sipping papaya juice, the wind chimes occasionally sprinkling their conversation with their pure and gentle chiming. The sun had long since set, and Rachel felt content and relaxed as she told the shack owner about her planned trip with Pravi.

'Looking for yourself in Mumbai?' Sarada had asked with a hint of an accent that Rachel couldn't quite place.

Rachel was swinging slightly in a hanging wicker chair, a glass of juice in her hand. Sarada cackled quietly to herself as she peered at Rachel over the top of a tall glass she was polishing. Rachel saw that her nails were rather dirty. She looked at her, frowning slightly. 'No,' she said. 'I just want to see a different place.'

'Different places, yes, you will find those if you look.' She laughed again.

'Do you know how long the train takes?' Gina asked.

'Two days at least. Indian trains.'

Rachel wondered if there was a hint of sarcasm in Sarada's voice. She couldn't decide whether she was being deliberately patronising or trying to sound enigmatic. They had only met her recently, here at the shack, but she had seemed friendly enough and the juice she served was delicious.

'Yes,' Rachel said carefully, 'but I want to see the city. I want to experience the bustle, the craziness. And I also want to go on a train journey. On an Indian train.' She held Sarada's gaze as she emphasised the word 'Indian'. 'I didn't come all the way to India to sit on the beach and buy trinkets. I want to experience the country.'

Sarada looked at Rachel for a long time, with something wistful about her, until Rachel laughed rather nervously and glanced at Gina, worrying faintly that she would take her comment as a slight.

They were interrupted by a fat, red-faced American man who bustled into the shack and kissed Sarada effusively on each cheek.

'Darling!' he said as Sarada hugged him. 'No, no, don't get me anything, I'm not staying. Friends of yours?'

He grinned widely at Rachel and Gina and waved his fingers at them. Without waiting for an answer, he said, 'Now look, Sarada darling, I am off to Delhi again. Get your butt over to my harbour place on Tuesday. You, my lovely, should look forward to a working shower and sleeping in a proper bed for a change!'

He winked at Rachel and Gina. 'My house-sitter,' he said, patting Sarada on one shoulder.

Sarada smiled warmly at him. 'Those comforts don't interest me,' she said, still smiling.

'Of course they don't darling. Now then, I am leaving Betty with you.'

He waved an enormous hand at a bright-blue, open-top jeep on the road outside. 'Be kind to her. I'll probably be about a week. No wild parties!'

The man laughed loudly at his own joke. 'And is the gorgeous Sarada looking after you?' he asked, looking at Rachel and Gina.

'Well yes...' Gina started to answer, but the man didn't wait for her to finish.

'Very dependable, despite the 'wild-woman-of-the-hills' thing she has going on.' He kissed Sarada on the hand as he said this.

Rachel and Gina smiled. 'Is Betty your car?' Rachel asked.

The man laughed. 'She sure is. And she's the love of my life! No one but Sarada here is trusted with her. Right then.' He kissed Sarada on each cheek again. 'The keys are in the usual place. I'll be back on the 9th. Enjoy!'

With that he jogged out of the shack and jumped into the jeep.

'Toodle-pip, one and all!' he shouted over the noise of the engine as he drove off amid a cloud of smoke. They could hear him laughing as he sped away.

'How old do you think Sarada is?' Rachel had asked later whilst combing out her hair in the bathroom of their hotel room.

'Quite a bit older than us, that's for sure,' Gina had called through the open door. 'Sixties, seventies?'

'Do you think so? She could be younger, with her wild hair and her nose stud.' Rachel looked at her own hair and fluffed it up, smiling at herself as she did. She came into the bedroom where Gina was sitting on her bed smoothing aftersun onto her pink legs. 'Caught the sun?' Rachel asked.

'Just a bit,' Gina replied. 'The sun only has to look at me and I'm damned well burnt to a crisp.'

Rachel climbed into her bed.

'It's a strange life she has, isn't it, living in that beach shack all by herself,' said Gina.

'At least she gets to house-sit in a proper place sometimes,' Rachel said. 'I wonder where she's from.'

'Ask her,' Gina replied, taking a last drag of her cigarette before grinding it out.

'She'd only give one of her weird, cryptic answers,' Rachel said.

'There is something odd about her. I think she might be lonely,' Gina said as she pulled up her thin cover.

'Mad more like,' Rachel answered.

At her shack, Sarada had suggested that Rachel and Gina fly to Mumbai together from Trivandrum. She came from behind her little wooden bar to sit with them on the balcony.

'There are regular flights. That might suit you better,' she said.

Gina looked expectantly at Rachel, but Rachel quickly shook her head.

'Look, I know the journey will be tough, but I'd regret not going by train. I'm interested in the train journey as much as in seeing Mumbai. I thought you were up for it, Gina.'

Gina didn't answer and Sarada once again looked at Rachel for a long time before asking, 'What is Pravi like?'

Gina was staring out across the sea and didn't look as though she were listening anymore. 'What?' she said. 'Sorry I was miles away.' She drained her drink. 'You don't have another one of these, do you?'

'Help yourself. It is all there behind the bar,' Sarada answered somewhat disconcertingly whilst still looking at Rachel.

'Sarada was asking about Pravi,' Rachel called to Gina as she walked to the bar.

'Oh Pravi, yes,' Gina called back. 'Well he's a nice guy, I suppose. Good fun. Of course we only met him last week,' she said rather pointedly as she returned holding a jug. 'Anyone else want a top-up?'

'There is a time for travel,' Sarada said as Gina went to make their drinks. 'There is a time for all things.'

'Well yes,' Rachel answered. 'And my time for travel is now.'

Rachel noticed that Sarada wasn't wearing shoes and felt momentarily and inexplicably annoyed at this.

'You know this is India,' Sarada said. 'It isn't like 'Fortress Europe' here. You might end up travelling much further than you intend.'

Rachel peered at Sarada, unsure of what she meant. She folded her arms in front of her, then unfolded them again not wanting to appear defensive. 'Sarada, I don't mean to be rude, but I have travelled before, you know.' She glanced at Gina who was slicing a lemon.

'I think you'll find,' Sarada said evenly, 'that what you are looking for is a little closer to home.'

Rachel frowned. 'I think that what I am looking for is an adventure,' she replied.

'Then I am sure,' Sarada said, 'that you will find one.'

Chapter 8 – Gina

By the pool Gina felt hot and sticky as she sat alone watching the other holidaymakers sunbathing and swimming, laughing and chatting quietly together. A residue of anger towards Rachel made her feel brittle and wretched, but she quickly reprimanded herself, telling herself to focus on her plans. She had decided to spend the morning at the hotel, swimming, reading perhaps. And then after lunch she'd go into Kanyakumari and find out about getting to the tiger sanctuary. She supposed she probably ought to try and find an internet café and email Richard, but her thoughts seemed far too big to reduce to mere words, and she didn't know what she would say to him. She didn't want to think, talk or write emails, but after the incident by the mirror Gina thought that she really ought to communicate with someone. She wished that Rachel were here so that they could go off and do something together and she wouldn't have to think. Once again her dream came to her unbidden and once again Gina struggled with it, trying to push it off.

The sun wanted to punish her, and as she stretched her legs out on the sunlounger she was aware of needing to look after herself. She picked up her sun cream and began to smooth it carefully into her limbs, her chest, her stomach. She liked the feel of the creamy white lotion against her hot skin as she rubbed it in lazily, making long strokes along her thighs and lingering on her abdomen. As she did so, she caught sight of a man sitting at the edge of the far side of the pool, watching her. He smiled when he saw that Gina noticed him. Gina looked away. She put her sun cream down on the ground and lay back on the lounger, the towel warm beneath her. She hadn't bothered with breakfast, other than the coffee she'd had on the balcony, and she wondered listlessly whether it was too early to order a gin and tonic. As she turned this thought around in her mind, she became aware of a shadow falling across her body. She opened her eyes to give her drinks order to the waiter but saw that it was the man from the far side of the pool. He was sitting himself down on the sunlounger beside her. *Oh no*, she thought, *here we go.*

'Hello,' the man said cheerfully, unintentionally sprinkling Gina with drops of water from his wet body.

'Hi,' replied Gina. She closed her eyes again, hoping that the man would see that she wasn't interested in him. The man ignored this and made a big show of getting himself comfortable on the lounger, adjusting his towel beneath him and stretching his hairy legs out in front of him. His sizable stomach fought with his blue trunks for supremacy. The trunks lost.

'I saw you were alone,' the man said, turning to Gina. He was British, from Kent or perhaps Essex, she guessed. 'So I thought I'd come and keep you company. I'm Dave.'

Of course you are, Gina thought.

'Gina,' she said, opening her eyes. She couldn't ignore him; it was too rude.

'Pleased to meet you, Gina.'

Dave leant across and held out a big wet hand. Gina took it for the briefest time she could.

'Your husband off sightseeing today is he then, Gina?' Familiar already, she thought.

'No, I'm here with my friend, but she's off sightseeing.'

Damn, Gina thought, cursing her lack of guile, why didn't she just let this man think she was married?

'Oh?' said Dave, clearly encouraged. 'So you really are all by yourself then.'

He stretched his big arms behind his head and looked up at the sky. I would be, Gina thought, if you'd leave me alone.

'Yup,' she said.

'Well we can't 'ave that, can we, a lovely young woman like you all on yer own.' He moved his head to one side and Gina heard a bone cracking. She wondered if he'd intended this. Dave turned to look at Gina.

'Lemme buy ya lunch, Gina,' he said. 'I know a quiet little place, not far from 'ere, overlooking the beach. It's beautiful.' He pronounced it 'bude if all'. 'Bude-if-all place, bude-if-all woman. Come on, Gina, Woj uh say?'

Gina looked at Dave. She supposed he was around thirty-eight, maybe forty. He had probably been a good-looking man once, and certainly he wasn't unattractive now. But he was, Gina thought as she eyed his hefty stomach, one of those brashly confident men whose past good looks encourage a persistently favourable view of themselves even after they have passed their physical best. Dave was solid and fat and had one of those pudgy red faces that would look very different were he still thin. He seemed an amiable enough chap, Gina thought, possibly even honourable. After all he'd ascertained that she didn't have a husband before he invited her for lunch. And Gina quite admired his self-assurance. She wondered why he was here alone. Perhaps his friend has gone to Mumbai, she thought, suppressing a sardonic smile. But the last thing she wanted now was to be alone with a man she didn't know. She decided that the best way to extricate herself from this situation was to lie.

'I'm sorry,' she said, forcing a smile to her lips, glad that she hadn't told Dave where Rachel had gone. 'But I'm meeting my friend for lunch. Perhaps another time.' And she sat up and started to collect her things together before standing to put on her sarong. Dave watched as Gina tied it around her waist, openly appraising her body, the little smile on his lips suggesting approval. Gina flushed deeply, feeling self-conscious and affronted, but she forced herself to smile politely and say goodbye as she headed off towards her room.

'Gina,' Dave called after her. 'You've left your sun cream here.'

Gina pretended she hadn't heard.

Back in the room, Gina wondered what she should do now. She had been planning to eat lunch at the hotel before going into town, but didn't want to encounter Dave, and in any case she didn't feel hungry. She looked at her watch and decided to have a quick coffee here in the room and then go into Kanyakumari. She cursed Rachel again, although part of her felt bad about doing so. They had planned on going to Mumbai together after all, and she knew how much Rachel wanted to go. Everything was fine, she thought, until that damned party on the beach. Gina sighed and picked up her cigarettes. For Christ's sake, she told herself viciously. Move on.

Chapter 9 – Sandrine

30th August 1967

My dear Perelle,

I arrived in the south after many days of travel, long and arduous. It has been some time since I wrote, and I have thought of you often. Madurai is cleaner than the cities in the north. And there are such temples, beautiful, ornate and colourful, very different from the Mogul architecture in the north. The big temple – Shri Meenakshee – was closed, but I walked all around it and then went into an indoor tailors' market, and I wasn't hassled as much as I was in the north. I have just been back to the Post Office (where they remembered my name) and have read your letter, which arrived at last. Give my best to Papa and wish him a speedy recovery for me. Of course I won't be cutting my trip short. I am sure that you will do an excellent job of caring for him throughout his recovery, which I am sure will be speedy. Perelle, I am concerned about your change in direction. Surely being a lecturer would be a good thing for you? And what background or training do you have in journalism? Think very carefully about this, Perelle. Although it pains me to say it, Papa is probably right, and you do need to find a direction and stick to it.

When I got back yesterday, my hosts told me that we were all going out to dinner, and they took me to a small restaurant which is just at the top of our street, where we ate dosa made with rice batter and black lentils, with coconut sambar. I will certainly miss them a great deal when I leave, which is very soon, Perelle. This morning

I got up early and had a mango for breakfast, which was soft, sweet and delicious. I was at the Meenakshi Temple before nine because it is so much cooler then and the crowds aren't so bad. The temple is in the town centre, a thirty-minute rickshaw ride away. It is huge and impressive – labyrinthine and so colourful. A lady in the temple put a bindi on my head and some flowers in my hair. Afterwards I went in search of mango juice. When I got back I asked the amma to explain all her spices and ingredients, which took a long time and was enjoyable. She made me taste lots of foods and spices. Some I knew and some I didn't. She fried a dried green chilli in hot oil and made me eat it, and my silly head nearly exploded, but it was delicious. She made a dal roti for lunch and showed me how, and I wrote down the recipe. I'll make it for you, Perelle, when I get home, if I can find all the ingredients. The appa showed me his flower and vegetable garden, which is by the house – he is very proud of it. He grows some of the things we eat, like coriander, fenugreek and chillies. After lunch I rested before my big trip. Perelle, you have the Post Office address there, so write me please, I implore you. It is so desperately important to me that I hear from you.

Chapter 10 – Rachel

The train arrived, a great screaming metal beast that groaned and shuddered and screeched to a long, painful halt. Rachel noticed that the carriages had the names of the passengers printed on thin, dirty sheets of paper which were stuck to the doors with yellowing sticky-tape that was already curling at the edges in the heat. Pravi told her that the names were all written in Hindi, and as he found their names on a carriage near the front, Rachel wished, not for the first time, that her digital camera hadn't broken the day they arrived in India. They climbed on board and Rachel felt a familiar jolt of exhilaration as she jostled along with Pravi and the other passengers to find their seats. It seemed that all the other passengers were Indian and she felt strangely pleased about this.

Rachel thought about Gina as she looked at Pravi, but quickly forgot about her in the heat and thrill of the moment, and she grinned like a child as the train lurched and groaned and began to move. Pravi looked back and fixed her with a quizzical stare, the corners of his mouth twitching upwards as though he were trying not to laugh. They sat on one long bench-seat under a window, one either end with their legs stretched out in front of them. There was a long curtain running the length of the seat, which later in the journey Pravi closed.

Rachel made herself comfortable, putting her backpack beside her and her sandals underneath the seat, and settled back to look out of the window. The glass was covered with a fine film of dust, and Rachel tried to wipe it clean with a tissue which she retrieved from her backpack, but couldn't because of course it was on the outside. Pravi watched all this in amused silence, raising his eyebrows and his shoulders in mock resignation when Rachel looked at him. She balled up the tissue and threw it at him. Pravi threw it back.

Their second-class carriage wasn't crowded, but there were people in most of the seats.

'The empty seats are all reserved,' Pravi told her. 'We were lucky to get ours at such short notice.'

Rachel thought back to how they had obtained their tickets as she looked around at the other passengers and wondered whether they were all used to offering bribes. She watched in fascination the people who were busily getting themselves comfortable in their places.

'Most Indians travel third class,' Pravi said. 'You wouldn't want to experience that. These are probably business people or the relatives of business people.'

Rachel noted the smartly dressed men on their own or in pairs shaking their newspapers out in front of them, some in western trousers and shirtsleeves, some in Indian dress, Punjabi pyjamas or long lungis. A man with sleekly oiled hair was talking loudly in Hindi on a mobile phone. He sounded angry to Rachel, but she had realised some time ago that she didn't always correctly identify the emotion behind Indian communication. A large middle-aged woman in a bright blue sari and lots of gold jewellery was explaining to some men in English why she always travelled by train. Cooler, more comfortable, she explained confidently and at length in a cutglass British accent that nevertheless had an Indian strum to it. Rachel smiled at the woman, who smiled back at her.

As they left the town and the journey got under way, Rachel's eyes were continually drawn to the window, and her first impression of the passing landscape was how deeply red it all was. The phrase 'burnt umber' sprang to her mind, and she thought of Indian women in brightly coloured saris. 'Everything is so vibrant in India,' she said to Pravi, not taking her eyes from the window. They began to pass lush fields, occasionally passing women and men bending to some work. They passed patches of trees, sometimes scrubby and sparse, sometimes larger, greener, more densely forested areas. The Cardamom Hills, a ridge of craggy but somehow gentle mountains contained the distance.

'Why are they called that?' Rachel asked.

Pravi laughed. 'Because the cool climate there is good for growing cardamom,' he answered. 'and coffee and pepper as well.'

The haze of the sunlight created a misty effect, which gave the mountains an air of fantasy. Everything was suffused by the interminable red of the earth, which, with the fulsome light of the sun pouring down on it all, seemed to breathe radiance and warmth into the whole moving scene.

As they rattled past the fields and forests, Rachel asked Pravi the names of some of the trees they passed. Pravi pointed out Banyans, Tamarind, Axlewood, Irul and Palm and it fascinated her that they were all different in both appearance and name from any trees that she was familiar with.

'Neem tree,' she repeated after Pravi. 'You know, I have never said that word before. I wonder if I typed the word 'neem' on my computer what the spellcheck program would want to replace it with.'

Pravi laughed loudly. But saying the word didn't help her to fix the meaning of the strange new trees. They remained strange, and Rachel stared out at them and marvelled.

Years before, when Rachel was at university, she had talked with one of her friends about going to India. They'd been walking by the campus lake, and as they'd gazed across its lightly dappled surface, watching the ducks bobbing their brightly coloured heads in and out of the water, they had talked about how exciting it would be to travel together. At that time she had never done what she thought of as travelling, and she resolved there and then to see something of the world beyond Europe, starting with India.

As they had wandered along, gathering their plans together, their words had seemed bright and buoyant and had skittered across the shallow lake like skimming stones. But the adventures they tried to create had been vague and romantic, and they plopped beneath the water almost immediately they were conceived. Rachel remembered her boyfriend of the time, an intense and possessive history student, who probably wouldn't have wanted her to go. Her friend had been scathing about this, and Rachel marvelled at her lack of responsibility, wishing that she too had the freedom to do as she pleased. She smiled at these recollections, congratulating herself on how much she had changed since then. She thought ruefully of Gina and how it had been her who had encouraged her to realise her dreams of travel. She really should be going to Mumbai with her.

But as she continued to stare out of the window she savoured the fact that here she was on a train clattering into Kerala towards Maharastra, the red earth and rocks, the wildly beautiful mountains and the strangely named trees right here and her here with them. She felt smugly glad that her possessive ex-boyfriend, her old university friend and that little, mocking undergraduate lake with its long-sunk skimming stones were all thousands of miles away. She felt acutely present in a way that she knew would be difficult to recreate in her memory. She wanted to breathe this place. She pulled her notebook out of her pack and wrote in it, 'I cannot think of anything more perfect than being on a train to Mumbai with Pravi.'

Chapter 11 – Sandrine

September 17th 1967

Perelle. I am back in Madurai. The trip to the coast was
fascinating. Rameswaram is an interesting town, on an
island, quite small amid beautiful coconut groves. It was
four hours away on a rattly old local bus along windy,
pot-holed roads. I shared a room with Asha, an
American who is from here originally, and we had some
very interesting talks about Hinduism which I found
intriguing. We were woken up at four each morning by
temple chanting, which we didn't mind at all. We visited
five temples which were all quite different, the big main
one being very impressive indeed with one thousand
pillars ranged along four corridors and with huge statues
of gods. I went for Dharshan, where you go and
worship the god and receive a blessing. The interesting
thing about that is that there were two queues – one for
free Dharshan (which was a very long queue) and one
for paying Dharshan, and that queue was very short, so
those with the means to pay get to receive their blessing
first. That didn't seem fair to me, but I paid anyhow as
we didn't have the time to queue in the free side. In one
of the smaller temples there were some priests in a sort
of a hole in the wall, and they told me to go and sit in
there with them, and so I did and we talked about where
I am from and what they were doing there in the hole,
but I didn't really understand what they were saying as
their English was so limited. I am fascinated, Perelle. I
plan to learn more about the religion here and what the

people believe. I feel more and more that there is something of note to find, something significant.

Mostly I didn't join the others for meals. I went for walks instead and ate bananas and drank tea, preferring to spend time alone with my thoughts. We went for a boat ride, which was rather uneventful as it didn't stop anywhere, but nonetheless it was a good chance to see some of the coastline, which was sandy and very pretty, flanked as it is by coconut groves. The main beach at the town is where people come to dunk themselves like at Varanassi, but there were no holy men like there were in Varanassi, bobbing in and out of the water as they performed their purification rites, only normally dressed people. We went to a different beach in a truck, which involved driving for about twenty minutes over sand along the seashore. It was exhilarating and the truck driver went quite fast. The beach was actually a sort of long, thin spit of land, which stuck out into the sea with water all around. It was very strange, as it looked like a kind of an island, as the way back was along a thin stretch of sand that you couldn't really see.

Perelle, I have talked at length in this letter about my most recent adventure. I am however, very much aware that I haven't addressed Father's concerns as conveyed via yourself in your last. I realise that Father isn't happy, and I remain grateful that in spite of this he continues to support me. But I am not coming home yet Perelle, and you must convey this to him. I therefore await news not of father's lack of imagination, but of your doings which I very much wish to hear about.

Chapter 12 – Gina

Pravi had been at the beach with them on that night. They'd been at a bar with him and a group of his friends and after a few drinks had decided to go to the beach. Gina couldn't remember now whose idea it was, but she suspected it was Pravi's. On the way they stopped at a small shop and bought some beers, a bottle of cheap local gin and some plastic cups from the surly, bored-looking vendor. They'd decided that it would be good fun to stay all night on the beach. Once there, more friends had arrived. She knew now that they were shack men, men who worked in the shacks by day and slept in them by night, as Sarada did. She wondered whether they were actually friends of Pravi's at all or just people he happened to know from the beach. But before long a party was in swing, with sunloungers pulled into a group, and singing in Tamil and in English, and people laughing and drinking and running to the sea and back. Rachel had sung a couple of songs, and although her voice wasn't outstanding, Gina had thought it was all very good fun, and she had laughed and clapped and joined in when the singing moved on to songs she knew.

Gina had been drinking the gin quite heavily and had started to be annoyed by Rachel. She couldn't quite remember why, but remembered it being something to do with Pravi and their incessant giggling. Her head hurt and she felt muggy and fuddled in her thoughts.

'I'm going for a walk,' she said to Rachel over the noise of the singing, 'Do you want to come with me?'

Rachel didn't hear her, engrossed as she was in the singing.

'Rachel,' she said again; 'I'm going to look at the sea.'

Rachel laughed loudly at something Pravi had said to her.

'I give up,' Gina muttered, stood up with her plastic cup and stumbled off. No one noticed her going and Gina hated them all for it. She gazed out at the gloomy water and then up at the equally gloomy sky, at the few stars that were visible amongst the high, dark clouds. She could hear the laughter and singing, and it felt to her that it was coming from a thousand miles away. As she stared at the undulating blackness in front of her, an intense loneliness rolled out from the sea and down from the blank sky. The barrenness of it felt physical and she could feel the sorrow pulling her abdomen.

In that moment, with the distant laughter taunting her and belittling her pain, the sky so vacant, lacking even the cold comfort of stars, Gina felt that if the sea came and swallowed her up she wouldn't care. She dropped to her knees and began to weep.

Rachel and Pravi found her lying on the sand, staring blankly up at the sky. Her tears had subsided but her wretchedness hadn't. Instead it had twisted itself into a dark, ugly rage. They helped her up and took her back to where the others were, and she didn't object. They said things to her that she supposed were meant to be consoling, but she wasn't really listening to their hollow words. Rachel hugged her a lot, which made her feel claustrophobic.

Inexplicably, someone brought over a little dog, a sandy-coloured mongrel, and sat it in Gina's lap. And Gina suddenly felt that here was a friend – something that would want her attention, would delight in her and in her stroking and petting and that wouldn't ignore her or assail her desolation with platitudes. And the little dog had indeed been content to sit in her lap and let Gina fuss over him. Gina announced that this dog was her true friend and that it was able to ease her pain when no one else could.

After that, the small group drifted apart – some settling down to doze on the sunloungers, some leaving to go to their homes. Gina's recollection of what happened next was dark and tangled. The men on the beach had said terrible things to her, things which distressed and horrified her. She recalled men all around her, calling and calling for Rachel, whom she couldn't see anywhere and who wouldn't come.

Gina supposed it must have been around four in the morning when they got back to the hotel. She had woken up around lunchtime feeling nauseous and headachy. She got up slowly, one hand steadying herself on the bed table, one to her head to ease buzzing and throbbing behind her eyes. She walked carefully through to the other room, steadying herself on the doorpost as she passed. Moving her head made her eyes hurt more. Rachel was on the balcony. Gina looked at her coldly through the French doors, pulling her silk dressing-gown tightly around her. She saw her cigarettes and lighter on the coffee table and picked them up; lit one with a shaking hand. She stared at Rachel for a few seconds more, sitting there on the balcony, all innocence. The word 'innocence' stuck in her parched throat, and Gina nearly retched. She went to sit next to Rachel.

'How are you feeling?' Rachel had asked.

Gina didn't have the words, all was hot, all was buzzing red and she couldn't contain it. 'How do you think I feel?' she spat. 'You left me on the damned beach with those men! Where the hell were you?'

'What do you mean?' Rachel had exclaimed, and Gina had felt a dangerous and frightening mix of rage and incredulity at the version of events that Rachel now dreamed up. Gina was astounded. She simply could not speak the things she felt, could not name them. She wanted to weep, but she couldn't. Some part of her wanted to tell Rachel, needed to tell her. But she couldn't. Her face felt red and puffy. Her throat felt dry and her head was still pounding. But although she knew what a bad state she was in, and that her memory of the night was muddled, this much she knew – Rachel had left her alone on the beach with those men.

Chapter 13 – Sandrine

21st September 1967

My dear Perelle,

I received your letter at last and your words bore me aloft! Tell Papa that I am well and am living perfectly well on my allowance. I have no need for more than I have. Perelle, you have given me what I most needed. The things you have bought me, keep them for now. I will not be returning soon, although I do thank you for thinking of me.

You said once, a long time ago, that when you see a woman you first look at her eyes and then her hair. Do you remember my eyes? What colour are they, Perelle? You should remember – they are blue like yours. And my hair, wild like yours. Not so easy to tame. And so, I wake here. I have opened my eyes, shaken out my hair, and I look to the day and to my continuing journey.

I am travelling with a somewhat dour Russian woman called Olga. We met on the train and have travelled together for a few days. We are together now as I write this at a small guesthouse near Coimbatorre. Olga and I have decided to go swimming later. There is a lake not far from here, by a hill that we can see from the guesthouse. This evening some of the other travellers we met in the town will get back from their travels – probably late. I had the room to myself last night, which I prefer, but I suppose I'll get used to sharing. Olga and I talked late into the night about yoga and Hindu mysticism. She had some fascinating things to tell me. She is interested in meditation. I have resolved to learn more. Perelle, you must talk to Papa for me. I am serious about extending my trip. I have so much still to see and to learn, even though I miss you, my darling brother. Tell me something about what you are doing, what books you have read and what friends you have seen. Your letters have become less frequent. Don't punish me, Perelle, although I am so very far from you, you are always with me and your letters are so important. I await your next with eager anticipation.

Chapter 14 – Rachel

For the first part of the journey Rachel felt transfixed, drinking in the rolling panorama, trying to imbibe the colours, the shapes, the feel of the place.

'Pravi,' she said, 'it's strange. I feel as though, unless I take in every little detail, the sense of being here will slip away from me. Do you know what I mean?'

Pravi smiled.

I am in India, she thought. It was miraculous to her, a bubble of time, place, and she in it. She felt a poignant sense of impermanence, that all this was fleeting, provisional, not quite real.

'I get the feeling that we can't inhabit anything if we are in transit,' she said, as much to herself as to Pravi. 'It's all too quickly gone.' As she gazed out of the dusty window, Rachel thought that she would be able to recall only the grand sweep, not the detail that she was seeing now. 'I think it is the detail that gives a place its being, you know, makes it authentic somehow. The detail is what people who don't live in a place notice.' Rachel had the notion that her separateness from this detail, her lack of connection to it enabled her to witness it but not to possess it. She had the sense that when she left India she would leave the detail behind her.

Rachel continued her reverie as she stared out at the rust-coloured Western Ghats in the distance. This red earth, she thought, belongs to Pravi. He owns it so completely, so intimately, that he doesn't even know that he owns it. They inhabit each other, Pravi in India, India in Pravi. And yet we can only own what is invisible to us. As soon as things become visible they assert their separateness and we lose them. If I am here, she thought, then inevitably everywhere else is there. Everyone one else is there.

Rachel looked at Pravi. His eyes were closed and he was leaning against the back of their bench, his long legs stretched in front of him, crossed at the ankles by hers. He was as strange to her as the neem trees. His skin was as rich and dark as the red soil, his tangled black hair as wild as these distant and impenetrable mountains. How can we really know anyone? she thought.

Pravi opened his heavily lashed eyes. He yawned luxuriantly and gave Rachel's bare foot a playful kick. Rachel smiled and pulled her legs up, crossing them in front of her. She reached into her backpack for her notebook and pulled it out, rummaged around and found her little silver pen, twisting the end to reveal the ballpoint tip. She opened the book at a blank page, and just as the train burst from a tunnel into glorious sunshine showering through the emerald trees, she wrote, 'Once upon a time there was a man named Michael.' Then she stretched across, gave the book and the pen to Pravi and watched as he read the sentence, seeing his wide mouth form into a child's grin before he laughed eagerly and stridently as she'd hoped he would.

If she cut the night on the beach in half and threw away the latter part, the evening had been perfect. Gina had taken some persuading, but had eventually agreed to go to the beach with the others. They'd arrived on the bikes, left them at the top of a softly sloping, sandy path and walked the short distance to a beach hut. Rachel had taken off her sandals and enjoyed the feel of the gritty sand beneath her feet. On the beach the guys arranged some sunbeds while she and Gina unpacked the carrier bag full of beer and gin, which they poured into plastic cups and started to hand around. They'd heard voices and some others came over from some way up the beach. There was much shoulder clasping and head-wobbling before the group settled on the sunloungers. Someone produced a guitar and began to sing an old Beatles song, and others joined in. Rachel joined in too and even felt brave enough to sing a couple of ballads herself – something she hadn't done for years. Everyone had clapped and Rachel had felt powerful and alive.

Someone began to sing 'Michael row your boat ashore', and both she and Gina sang along loudly, swaying from side to side in time to the song. After, Rachel asked of no one in particular, 'Who is Michael, anyhow?' and what followed was a ridiculously earnest exchange about Michael, who he was, what he was doing in a boat and why he had to row it ashore. Rachel shrieked with laughter and noticed that Pravi was laughing enthusiastically too, and this spurred her on to ever wilder speculations about Michael and his aquatic antics. The tale eventually died away and someone struck up another song, but as the group were singing, Pravi prodded Rachel in the arm and whispered 'Michael!' and Rachel collapsed again into fits of stifled giggling, and they continued in this vein as though 'Michael' were a code word for something hilarious that only they understood.

Rachel hadn't been particularly aware of Gina, but suddenly realised that she wasn't there. She looked around and couldn't see her and assumed she must have gone off to find a quiet spot to relieve herself. But she was taking too long and after a while Rachel stood up and looked around. Surely that wasn't Gina lying by the sea?

Rachel narrowed her eyes as she stepped over the bags strewn around them. She walked briskly and deliberately over to Gina. Pravi got up and followed her. She squatted down beside her, feeling a slightly guilty repulsion as she looked at Gina's flushed and swollen face. She looked as though something vital had drained away from her. 'Gina?' she said. Gina didn't respond. 'Gina, come on, sit up.' Gina stared at the sky and didn't move. Her face was wet and there were tears making tracks down her cheeks. An empty paper cup was lying in the sand. Rachel stared at her. She felt as though she didn't know how to rescue Gina from this darkly emotional place. 'For goodness sake, Gina,' she muttered, closing her eyes for a few seconds. 'Come on,' she said. 'You can't lie here by the sea on your own like this. Sit up.'

Pravi helped her to stand Gina up, and together they led her back to the sunloungers. As they sat her down, Gina began to cry again. Rachel stared at her and wondered why she had done this, why she was attention-seeking in such a way. 'It's okay,' she said to the group. 'It's just the drink.' But Rachel felt a burden of obligation to articulate something nurturing, and although she said things to Gina that she hoped were comforting, she suspected that her conflicting feelings might prick the authenticity of her words and leave them flat and empty.

The singing had subsided and the others in the group now sat around, some looking uncomfortable. Suddenly one of the group appeared with a little dog, which he gave to Gina. An inspired idea, Rachel thought, something to focus on, to take the attention off Gina's morbid introspection. 'Look at this cute little thing,' she said as Gina took the dog. But when Gina told her to leave her alone, that the dog was more her friend than she was, Rachel jerked her head up in surprise and was about to make some retort when Pravi stood up and indicated with a tilt of his head that she should follow him.

They wandered together down to the water's edge, where the waves seemed to be taking their incessant anger out on the shore. They walked along in silence a little way until Pravi headed up the sand and pulled up two sunloungers. They both sat down. Rachel looked over at the group of friends and was pleased to see that Gina and the others seemed to be talking, although she couldn't hear what they were saying. She looked at Pravi and started to say something about Gina needing a lot of attention, but Pravi put his finger on her lips. He looked at Rachel for a long time before lying back on his lounger and staring up at the sky. Rachel looked at his body, stretched taut, his arms flung behind his head in a gesture of comfortable abandon. She looked at the contours of his chest beneath the white cotton of his loose shirt, the strip of dark flesh where the shirt had risen above the waist of his jeans. She swallowed and looked quickly away, turning instead to look at the harmless sea. She felt her heart pounding as she stared into the dark before she too lay back on her lounger.

Suddenly Rachel started and sat up. Pravi was standing up, adjusting his shirt. 'Come on, quickly,' he said and turned and walked back towards where the party had been. Rachel stumbled after him feeling muzzy and chilly. Most of the group were gone by now, but Gina was staggering about, and three of the men seemed to be trying to make her sit down. One of them was trying to put a towel around her shoulders, but it was clear that Gina didn't want either the towel or to sit down. The dog was nowhere to be seen.

Rachel took a deep breath, focused on waking herself up and marched over, grabbing their bags on the way. She saw that Gina was half-gulping, half-crying, and when she saw Rachel, her eyes widened and she sobbed that she wanted to go home. Rachel took another deep breath and, with silent resignation, calculated in her head how long it would take to walk back to the hotel – fifteen minutes at most she thought. Pravi was standing by Gina looking worried and uncomfortable. And there was something else in his face that Rachel couldn't quite name.

'I'll deal with this Pravi,' she said. 'I'll take her back to the hotel.'

Pravi wasn't convinced. 'I am not sure that is wise, Rachel. I will take you.'

'Honestly, Pravi, I'll never get her onto a bike in this state. Please, just let me deal with her. The hotel isn't far.'

'Well then, I will walk you back,' Pravi replied.

'Please Pravi, thanks, but I don't need your help.'

Eventually he walked reluctantly back to where the three men were standing in a group. Rachel heard him talking quietly to them in Tamil as she put her arm around Gina's shoulder and led her stumbling up the beach towards the path.

Somehow Rachel managed to get Gina back to the hotel, Gina stumbling and uttering thick and muggy objections, Rachel holding on to Gina's shoulders and guiding her forward, trying to steady Gina's swaying gait with her hip. It wasn't a long walk, and once there and safely in their room, Rachel focused on getting Gina out of her clothes and into bed.

'Honestly, Gina,' she muttered as she got the plastic bucket from the bathroom just in time and, turning away and closing her eyes, held Gina's hair back as she bent over it, heaving and retching. 'That's it, you'll feel better after,' she said.

When it seemed as though Gina wasn't going to be sick anymore, Rachel fetched a bottle of water and made Gina drink some of it. The light at the edges of the window shutters told her that the sun was just coming up.

The next morning Rachel woke late and, seeing that Gina was still asleep, crept quietly out of the room and made herself some tea. On the balcony, barefooted and still wearing her nightshirt, she absently watched a young Indian man sweeping the red-tiled path in the heat. As she sipped her tea, she thought through the events of the night and once again felt acutely aggrieved that Gina had spoilt the evening. Rachel hoped that she would feel suitably contrite when she finally got up. She felt a sense of martyred pride as she considered how she had comforted her friend and how she had managed to get her back to their hotel by herself and look after her so well.

Rachel started in surprise as Gina stepped onto the balcony. She had expected her to be asleep for most of the morning. Gina looked dishevelled and grey, and as she sat down, Rachel asked her how she was feeling. Gina's reply hit her like a slap.

'Gina,' she said, 'I don't know what you think I did wrong. Don't you remember me helping you, getting you from the sea when you were crying? Getting you home? You were completely wasted. Christ, you were nearly sick all over me!'

'I don't know why you went off with Pravi and left me there with those men.'

'Gina, I didn't go off with Pravi. I was right there on the beach. I could see you!' Rachel forced herself to speak more quietly. 'I've never seen you like this, Gina,' she said as she got up and went inside.

She stood in the kitchen for a few moments, calming herself before putting the kettle on. She came back to the balcony a few minutes later with coffee for Gina, who took it without meeting her eye. Rachel sat and sipped her tea in silence.

On the train, Pravi held Rachel's notebook very seriously and seemed to be considering something of great import, his eyes boring into the yellowing ceiling of their carriage as though there he might find the extraordinary thing that he was searching for. Then, with one eyebrow raised, he looked at Rachel for a moment before flourishing her silver pen extravagantly and writing something in the book. Then, with a grin that crinkled the corners of his eyes and made Rachel think of a bridge, he stretched across the space between them and handed the book and the pen back to her. Their light hilarity sparkled around them as they bounced Michael back and forth, sending him on all sorts of nautical adventures, which always ended in some disaster, with Michael's friends on the beach shouting for him to row his boat ashore. The pair shook and wept with laughter as Michael's new exploits colonised more and more of the notebook, and the other passengers in the train frowned or smiled or looked away as their natures dictated.

Chapter 15 – Sandrine

11th October 1967

My dear Perelle,

I had a wonderful trip to the coffee plantation with a Spanish photographer called Pablo. It was beautiful – high up in the mountains at a place called Thandikuddi. The Indian couple who run it were inspirational. They mainly employ widows so that they can offer a home and security to them, and they often pay for the education of their children. They invited us to dinner at their private lodging, and we had some excellent conversations about Indian life and most particularly religion. It seems that here one cannot separate one from another. They have invited me to their farm, which is closer to Madurai, and I would like to go, but I'm not sure I have the time as soon I must journey on.

One evening recently, four of us arranged a party for some children in an orphanage. There were about forty of them and we took food and cakes. Their situation was dire. There was almost no furniture and the children all slept together in one big room on the floor. They eat their food outside on the ground with chickens and goats roaming around, pecking them. But they were such happy children – they put on a little show for us, which included dancing and singing and yoga demonstrations. They don't have shoes to wear, so I am buying them all sandals. I was taken to the house of a doctor the other day, and I met his two children. The girls were bright and receptive, and the contrast between their situation and that of the orphans was stark.

I marvel at the lack of interest in material things here, even the house of the doctor, though large and well built, was not very well appointed, the furniture basic and with a minimum of ornamentation. It inspires me and makes me think about what is important in my own life. I recently went for a hike up to a temple on top of a hill not far from the house where I am staying. It was a good walk with wonderful views across the sprawling town to the east and cucumber fields to the south, the distant hills wreathed in purplish mist. I made the mistake of taking some bananas out of my backpack to eat on top of the mountain, and I was surrounded by monkeys! I looked down over the town and the fields, and I felt something strange – a kind of connection to all that I was seeing. As though I were somehow a part of it all. The rains started when I got back down into the village that night, and it was an utter deluge – I had to shelter in a doorway before I found a rickshaw. I have never seen rain like it. The roads became rivers, and there were bicycles swamped and floating about – the water was up to the tops of the wheels of the rickshaws, and it was so frightening that I almost couldn't look. The storm had retreated over the hills by the time I got back to the house. I watched the distant lightning from the rooftop. It was beautiful, and I almost felt like staying. But of course I must journey on.

Chapter 16 – Gina

Gina's outburst had left her feeling stunned and upset in the same way that toddlers are often shocked by the ferocity and power of their tantrums. She'd had no idea that she had it within her to react so strongly and she felt drained and hollow. After Rachel had brought her a cup of coffee she'd sat there for what felt to her like a long time, not really thinking, but following in her mind fragments of images that didn't fully make sense and that she didn't want to see. She'd forced herself to banish them, scolding herself like a child. She had drunk her coffee and faced Rachel, who had been sitting in silence, balancing her cup on her knee as she stared over the balcony to the path below.

Gina thought of this now as she sat in the internet café in Kanyakumari, trying to decide what to say to Richard. She had made her peace with Rachel. They had agreed to make a fresh start and get on with their trip. Gina wanted to forget the evening, to wipe it from her memory. She knew though that she had to send some communication to Richard.

Hi Rich

She put her hands in her lap, twisting her thumb into her fist. What could she say to him? She didn't know where to begin and was sure that she would sound false whatever she said. Besides, she thought, how could she bare her soul in an email? Her mind flashed back to when she was an English undergraduate at Warwick, faced with a difficult essay. Her personal tutor had given her the advice that whenever she found herself in this predicament she should simply begin to write, not thinking or worrying about whether what she was writing made any sense. The advice had stood her in good stead, and she'd always managed to produce passable essays, so now, in the hot and sticky café, under the flickering fluorescent lighting, she began to type.

I am emailing from an internet café in Kanyakumari. I didn't mail you before because I didn't come across an internet café and anyhow we have been so busy. It's a billion degrees outside and even more in here, so you are lucky that I am sitting here long enough to send even this! I am having a great time. Even better than Thailand. Rachel and I have done all sorts of exciting things and have hooked up with some fun people. We've been to temples and ruins and the old town and loads of bars, and we even had a party on the beach with our new friends, which was fabulous, and we didn't come home all night. Rachel and I sang and everyone loved us.

Gina looked at what she had written. Well, it was mostly true; there was no denying that. She continued, vaguely enjoying the sound of the keys clacking as she hit them.

You've never heard me sing, have you? I have a great voice. Everyone on the beach said so. So you were wrong about me coming here, and it certainly was the right thing to do. Your email was conspicuously absent, but I suppose I forgive you. I know you are upset that I came.

She re-read what she had typed. She didn't like it but decided to leave it as it was. She ploughed on, jabbing more insistently at the keyboard as she typed, as though the strength of her typing could somehow find its way into the words themselves.

Rachel is well and sends her love. She is finding the heat hard work but apart from that is fine and having a ball as she always does. We've done so many fantastic things together. One of the people we have met here is a musician. We have seen quite a bit of

67

him and his friends. I think Rachel is soft on him. Maybe I am soft on him too. Are you jealous? That I have met a nice Indian man? You should be. Maybe he likes me. Perhaps I'll stay here and live with him. Why haven't you emailed me? I thought you might at least have sent me a line, just to wish me well, to ask how I'm coping. You're punishing me, aren't you?

Damned garbled rubbish, she thought, and deleted the whole paragraph, stabbing at the delete key so forcefully that the man at the counter looked up and frowned. She felt angry with herself now. Surely she could say something meaningful to the man she shared her life with?

Anyhow, I am having a marvellous time here. I'm fine and I'm enjoying my break. We're off to a tiger sanctuary soon. We are planning how to get there. Are you going to be at the airport when I get back? I wish you would email me. Just tell me things are okay. That this hasn't driven us apart. You knew I wouldn't change my mind about coming here. It wasn't fair of you to ask. So please email me. Right I'm off to plan this trip. Hugs and email me. Soon. I mean it. Bye xxx

Gina clicked the send button quickly. This out of the way, she could get on with the rest of her day. She felt faintly guilty about thinking of Richard in this dismissive way, but she knew too that she couldn't open up to him in an email. She would talk to him when she got home in person and in private, not sitting in a dirty internet café with other computer users wandering in and out, possibly taking furtive glances at what she was typing. Richard needed to hear from her, to know that she was having a good time. This, she thought, was enough for now.

Chapter 17 – Sandrine

24th October 1967

Darling Perelle,

Firstly I really must tell you off for your lack of communication. I haven't received a single word from you for really quite some time. Have you forgotten your dear sister? Write me soon, I insist. I have had a rather dramatic morning. I went swimming at seven at the lake with only a few rupees left to my name. I wasn't worried as I was told that I could access my allowance at a place in town, so I paid the rickshaw man to take me to the lake and then to town, but I discovered that the place wouldn't allow me to access any money. So, the rickshaw man agreed to take me to another place about fifteen minutes away. We peddled there only to find that the place didn't open until ten o'clock. So, there I was with no money and a rickshaw man to pay. I told him to take me back to my guest-house so that I could borrow some money from someone – happily James was there – an interesting American man who works for a charity – and he lent me some money. It means that I have to go all the way back into town later to get my allowance money. But it's all experience isn't it? I shall make sure that I don't run short in future.

Later. I went back into town to get my money, and I couldn't find the place. Eventually I spotted a place I thought might be able to help. I asked someone and I was directed up some dark stairs to a dingy looking room. I told them what I wanted and they told me to wait. Eventually a stern-looking man came and did the transaction. I withdrew it all, Perelle, because, although I realise how vulnerable that makes me to thieves, I would rather that than risk be stranded here without means. Please tell Papa. After this I decided to get the bus back, but I couldn't find the right road after walking for a long time, so I decided to get a rickshaw after all. But none of the rickshaw men could understand where I wanted to go, so eventually I asked for the name of the lake. When I told him to stop before we got to the lake, the man tried to charge me too much, but I made him agree to a compromise. On Monday I leave for Kanyakumari. It is a remote place at the end of the world, and I am hoping to meet a holy man there whom Olga told me about. I am hoping that I can learn meditation from him and more about the Hindu religion. I don't know how long I will be there for. It depends on whether I find this man.

Chapter 18 – Rachel

It delighted Rachel that, throughout the journey, men would walk up and down the carriages of the train calling out the various foods and drinks they had to sell. The men rattled off the often mystifying names of their wares at a baffling speed, their voices somehow both indifferent and insistent. Each man appeared to serve only one dish, but there was a huge array of dishes available, which meant a great number of men walking up and down the carriage in a constant babble of culinary calling. It almost sounded religious, Rachel thought, as strange names were intoned and chanted over and over – *batatawada, dahiwada, idli sambar, gulab jamun, rasgulla, chickeey, chai* – like mantras that would bring enlightenment or peace or both. It appeared that you could buy almost anything you might wish to consume in the train – fruits and nuts, tomato soup, rice, yoghurt, chicken, dahl, roti, coffee, juices of all kinds, and of course the ubiquitous chai. Drinking a cup of the hot, spicy tea, Rachel asked Pravi about each of the dishes on offer. She was surprised and delighted that the food of India was richer, more varied and more refined than the 'Indian' food she ate at home from local curry houses. 'You know Pravi,' she said, 'back home we eat a lot of what we call curries. Our Indian restaurants are full of endless generic Baltis and Kormas, but they all taste the same and they are nothing like the food here.'

The smells that accompanied the food vendors on their journey through the carriages were as captivating to Rachel as the names and the nature of the foods themselves. Rachel immersed herself in the subtly spicy, aromatic sensuality of the experience. At times the scents were piquant, peppery, fiery, at others pungent and heady. Citrus and coffee mingled with cumin, garlic, ginger cardamom and chilli, which together created a complex blend of spiciness, richness and sweetness which appeared and disappeared, melded and separated with a quiet stealth that seemed quite independent of their source. These aromas felt to Rachel heavily charged with the promise of the exotic, of difference, of 'otherness'. She closed her eyes, letting the fragrances of these strange foods assume a presence which enveloped her, touched her body, infused her mind. In their mysteriousness, she drew from them evidence of her adventuring, questing nature and the fact that she was a long way from home.

Pravi asked Rachel whether she was hungry yet. Rachel considered this, balancing the enticing nature of the food against the possibility of dirty cooking conditions on the train, of murky water that the utensils and foods might have been washed in and prepared with, but she managed to banish these finger-wagging thoughts with the comforting knowledge of the Ciprofloxacin in her backpack.

They ate matka dahi. The attentive young man who had called out the name of his wares handed her a small, crumbly clay pot, which contained a whitish substance with a watery surface. It looked like fresh, natural yogurt. Pravi watched in a faintly amused way as Rachel peered inside the pot before sniffing at it. Rachel wondered whether this taste sensation was what the Japanese call 'umami', but remembered vaguely that umami was associated with savoury tastes.

'I can't decide whether I like it or not,' she said to Pravi. 'It's slippery. I think I like it though because it is different.'

Pravi smiled. '*Atithi Devo Bhava*,' he said, and looked at Rachel intently.

Rachel smiled and raised her eyebrows.

'*Atithi Devo Bhava*,' Pravi repeated. 'A guest is equal to God.'

Rachel nodded her understanding and looked at Pravi. He seemed to enjoy introducing her to the local foods and drinks and behaved like an attentive host, patiently trying to find the right English words to describe what Rachel was experiencing.

Later, Pravi closed the long curtain so that they were in a thin space that created the feeling of privacy. Outside, the light was softening to a muted orange glow. Rachel looked out of the window. She watched two colourfully dressed young women carrying baskets of long, thin sticks on their heads along a track through a dry field. Their brightly coloured saris echoed the colour of the soil beneath their feet so that it seemed as though they were wearing the landscape itself. The phrase 'the embers of the day' popped into Rachel's mind, and she briefly pondered where she had heard it. She craned her neck to see the sunset, but realised that they were on the wrong side of the train. She looked back at the women, and as the train clattered past them leaving them to their world, Rachel wondered where they were going and what they would do when they got there. She felt a sudden and irrational wave of loneliness and wished that she could be with these women, chatting easily after whatever toils they had completed and going back to prepare a meal for their menfolk and children and to enjoy more companionship. Instead she was the traveller, the guest – held aloft, equal to God, but alone. As the light faded, she wondered if it were true that people who travel are searching for home, and if so why they often favour countries and cultures that are so different from their own – places where they couldn't possibly find a 'fit', places where they would always be the outsider.

Rachel lay back in the long seat and stretched her legs out in front of her, flexing her bare feet. The thigh of her right leg settled against Pravi's, and the hard, warm, male contact both comforted and thrilled her. She stuffed her backpack behind her head to make a pillow and closed her eyes.

As Rachel's breathing became slower and shallower, scents of spices and fruits and chai wrapped around her, and images of the women in the field stole into her mind and gradually began to mingle with thoughts of Gina. Her thoughts drifted and floated with the heady aromas in the train and lured her into a warm, red field where the sun was setting. It was dinner-time, and she and Gina were supposed to be guests at a meal. They could smell the food and Rachel was hungry, but they were searching for something and she didn't know what. Gina was distraught, and as the setting sun cast its last translucent rays and darkness overcame them, she started to cry and tried to tell Rachel something about the men who were standing at the shadowy edge of the field. But Rachel couldn't hear what Gina was saying because she was listening to someone far away who was chanting something magical into the darkness. Rachel tried to follow the sound of the chanting, first slowly and then running through the dark field, but the chanting got further and further away until it was very faint. Rachel stopped running and turned to find Gina, but she'd left her behind, and although she realised that the sound she could faintly hear was Gina crying, she found herself on her own in the dark field.

Chapter 19 – Sandrine

13th November 1967

Dearest Perelle,

A letter from you! Time passes so quickly as you say, and I agree. I have found the holy man, and he has interested me in yoga. I arrived here some days ago and at first had no clue how to find the yogi. Eventually I was told of a holy man living in a remote place by the sea. I took the bus with a Dutch woman who said she had been there before but couldn't remember the name of the place, only what it looked like, so we had to try and explain that to the bus man, which was amusing with the other passengers all joining in trying to help. We managed with their help to get off at the right stop somehow, and I am happy to say that the yogi was indeed a wizened, white-bearded and sweaty-looking man at least one hundred years old as I had hoped and expected. He was wonderful – full of humour and grace. We did yoga in a thatched room with statues of gods all around, to the sounds of gentle chanting. The yoga itself was very good. I went to the place again this morning at seven. We did yoga practice once more underneath the thatched roof, the incense scenting the air. It made me feel very calm. On the way back I had to hang out of the door of the bus with a gaggle of others doing the same thing because everyone was going to work by that point and the thing was bursting at the seams.

Days later. It is very early and people are beginning to wake. I am starting to see a common humanity here.

Out of sleep people begin to collect their concerns around them and me mine. We aren't so very different, after all. Perelle, can you hear me? You don't know where I am, I know. Do you wonder? Are you thinking of me? I was looking at a map and counting off all the places I have been. It seemed to me akin to Papa's trophy cabinet, the counting akin to polishing the trophies. It made me feel solid in the world, Perelle, to know that I have been to some of it. But there is so much more! I can't stop now. Tell Papa I won't be returning yet.

Chapter 20 – Rachel

'You told them what?'

Rachel was round-eyed and alert in her astonishment.

'I told them that she is a mother,' Pravi repeated.

Rachel looked at him in disbelief. 'You told them she is a mother?'

'Yes.'

'But why? Why would you make up such a lie? She isn't even married. Where are her children?'

'Western women are different from Indian women. Mothers here are sacred, held in high esteem and respected.'

Since she woke, sweating and aching in the dimly lit carriage, Rachel had been thinking about what had happened at the beach party. Something was nagging at her, something disturbing in her dream, and the more she thought, the more her apprehension grew. Pravi was sleeping in his own bunk above, and alone in the half light Rachel thought about the men in her dream, standing there at the edge of the field, and the men on the beach. She thought about the events of that night – Pravi calling her, Gina crying, frightened, the men huddled in a group. Did she remember seeing them pulling at Gina when she and Pravi were returning from along the beach? She couldn't be sure what was memory and what she was imagining.

She tried to tell herself that she was being silly, there had been nothing to worry about on the beach, nothing worse than Gina getting drunk and morose. She'd had a strange dream, that was all. But even so, thoughts of the shadowy figures of the men wouldn't leave her.

Rachel felt movement in the bunk above and heard Pravi yawning before clambering down and stretching his arms above his head. Rachel swung her feet to the floor and begun to fold her sheet, glad to be distracted from her thoughts.

'I trust you slept well in your five-star accommodation,' Pravi said with a wink.

'Sort of,' Rachel replied, smiling thinly. 'I'm a little stiff. I think I'll go and freshen up.'

Pravi nodded. 'You do that,' he replied. 'I will go and find you some nice hot chai. You will feel better.'

Back at their seat, chai in hand, Rachel looked at Pravi, who was trying to find something in his backpack. She was reluctant to raise the issue with him, but she wanted reassurance. 'I'm not making an accusation,' she said. 'Of course, they are your friends and I'm sure everything was fine. It's just that Gina seemed a bit upset.'

Pravi nodded slowly and fixed her with an intense stare. He seemed to be saying to her that he had deliberately told his friends that Gina had a child so that, if he and Rachel found themselves with an opportunity to be alone, Gina would be respected. 'Trust me, Rachel,' he said, 'no harm came to Gina from those men.'

Rachel nodded back. She tried hard to remember what she had seen when she came up the beach to take Gina home. Gina staggering around the beach, the men all around her.

'They are good men. Friends, Rachel. I have known them long.'

Pravi's light, unconcerned certainty jarred with Rachel's foreboding. She desperately wanted his words to rescue her, but was he simply saying what she wanted to hear? This is silly, she told herself. She took a deep breath and then another. She looked out of the window, but in the thick dust all she could see was her own grim reflection, drawn and tired. She tried to think back to how Gina's clothes had looked when she took her back to the hotel and when she undressed her. She couldn't remember anything that might have alarmed her. She didn't recall that Gina's clothes were dishevelled or torn. In their argument on the balcony, Gina had accused Rachel of leaving her alone on the beach with the men. After the argument, they had carried on as though the night hadn't happened, trying to be natural with each other. But something had changed. The question Rachel asked herself now was how significant was the thing they were choosing to ignore? Had Gina been raped on the beach that night?

There. She had articulated the stalking word. And here she was on a train travelling hundreds of miles to Mumbai, having left her friend behind on her own. Maybe (oh please, she thought, please) if nothing had happened on the beach other than drunken melancholy, the break would give them both some perspective. But Rachel forced herself to contemplate an uglier hypothesis: that Gina had been assaulted on the beach that night by a group of men, and she had left her on her own to deal with it. Rachel felt sick and headachy. Christ, she thought, what have I done?

Rachel looked at Pravi, who was examining her with an unfathomable expression that frightened her. His characteristic half-smile looked more like a sneer now, a leer. She didn't know this man. She knew almost nothing about his life, other than what he had elected to tell her. And yet she had chosen to trust him, to leave her friend and embark on a four-day trip with him to a foreign city she had never been to and where she knew no one. Rachel thought grimly about Gina's warnings. She looked around her and saw nothing familiar to calm her, to reassure her. Suddenly, Rachel didn't know what she was doing, where she was going. She was alone with this stranger on her way to some faraway place, and Gina was alone in Kanyakumari. Rachel wanted to be with her, to hug her, to comfort her, be comforted by her, to know that here was someone she knew, who she trusted.

She curled herself into her corner of the seat, hugging her knees to her chest, trying to give Pravi the impression that she was simply tired. She thought about Sarada's words: 'It isn't like fortress Europe here.' The words had annoyed her at the time. Now she wondered about her own situation and whether she had been naive to trust Pravi after all. But, she told herself, although Pravi was a stranger to her, nothing in anything he had so far said or done had caused her to doubt him or to think that she could come to any harm with him. He presented himself as gracious, thoughtful and kind, and unless he was playing a very clever and manipulative game, then he was simply an adventurous young man who had taken the opportunity to spend some time with a similarly adventurous young woman. Surely, Rachel thought, this is normal? In which case she ought to trust what he said about his friends on the beach, that their culture dictated that Gina, a mother as they thought, was to be revered, elevated above any advances they might otherwise have considered making. This was what Pravi was asking her to believe. And he knew these men.

He said that, in any case, they were good people, trustworthy friends.

Rachel took a deep breath and sat up. This really is stupid, she thought as she pushed her hair out of her face and re-tied her ponytail. She looked into Pravi's open face. His eyes were closed and he looked younger than his twenty-eight years. He looked like a boy – small, defenceless. Yes – she trusted him. She told herself that she had panicked unnecessarily because of her stupid, meaningless dream. She had never before considered that dreams had any meaning, and she certainly wasn't going to imbue this one with meaning now. She would stick to the facts. If Gina had been assaulted, she told herself firmly, she would not simply have gone on with their holiday as though nothing had happened.

Rachel stretched her arms above her head and yawned. She had been travelling all day and all night, she hadn't eaten properly, she felt grubby and she was aching and tired. She would think about Gina again later on, after a night's sleep in a proper bed, when she was rested, and when her head was clear. After all, she was on her way to Mumbai. She was with Pravi. She was having fun.

Later that day, before the sun set again, Rachel grabbed her day bag and followed Pravi, swaying and lurching through the carriages to the toilet compartment. She came out of the tiny room holding her breath and trying not to gag, thanking all the powers that she could muster for the fact that she had brought her own toilet paper and baby wipes. Pravi was waiting for her by the midsection carriage door. It was open. Rachel panicked briefly, looking up and down the carriages, thinking that they would get into trouble with the train guard for opening the outer door. But she quickly reminded herself that this was India and whatever she considered the normal rules to be didn't necessarily apply here. She dumped her bag on the floor and stood opposite Pravi, leaning against the carriage wall, her hand on a rail on the side-wall. She stared out of the gap at trees, a stream, small hills as they rushed past in a blur of green and red. She pulled the band from her hair and put it around her wrist as she shook her hair out, with the intention of tidying and refastening it. As she did so and without warning, Pravi launched himself out of the carriage, hanging onto his handrail with one hand and holding out his free arm to the rushing air, laughing and shouting. Rachel laughed and without thinking gripped her rail tightly, planted her feet hard on the floor and flung herself out of the carriage door. Her hair was snatched away by the hot wind and whipped wildly behind her, and she felt her heart pumping riotously as she screamed and laughed, the pair of them hanging out of the carriage, waving their free arms manically as the train clattered noisily over a viaduct. In this singular, perilous moment vitality and life coursed through her and Rachel's optimism told her in that second to trust that she would be okay. When they pulled themselves back into the carriage, they both laughed honestly and dangerously, and Rachel felt that she recognised something untamed in Pravi – something she had sensed the day they had met – the same feral, trusting thing which she felt in herself and which allowed such acts of abandon.

Chapter 21 – Gina

Gina hadn't expected to be abandoned in India, and as she stood forlornly outside the internet café wondering which way to go, she felt small and lost amid the clamour and dash of the weekday town. She sighed and took her bag from her shoulder. Gina had bought the bag for a bargain price a few days ago from a street stall by the temple, and she liked the embroidered red cotton, the vivid threads and little mirrors that adorned it. 'Red,' Rachel had said. 'The colour of life.' And Gina had agreed. She rummaged around in the bag until she found her cigarettes and her lighter, lit one and took a long, deep, grateful drag. She hung the long cotton strap of her bag over her shoulder and looked around her. One of the tiny mirrors sewn onto the bag flashed in the sun.

If this were a film, Gina thought, blowing smoke from her pursed lips into the waiting air, she would look up and see some handsome man she knew rounding the corner, coming her way. He would see her and wave in surprise, call her name and hurry over, smiling to ask what she was doing. He would be pleased to hear that she had no fixed plans and would persuade her to join him for lunch. They would walk together through the busy town, he pointing out places of interest (this Hindu temple, and look, across the street a museum dedicated to Gandhi, how fascinating!) They would eventually choose a secluded water-front restaurant, would marvel at the view (so beautiful, look at statue out in the bay, the pale sand, the sapphire water, surely nowhere like it in the world!) dally over the menu choices (fresh fish, or this exotic salad, it all looks so good!) They would linger over a bottle of wine, both of them trying to stretch out the afternoon, enticing one another with teasing little tales, all of which beckoned towards unspoken bedroom conclusions. Back at his hotel they would watch the setting sun fling rubies over the shimmering sea, drinking a dangerous crimson cocktail (and another, why not?) on a moonlit balcony before moving hand in hand to the bedroom.

But as Gina stood there despondent in the mundane clamour and rush of the afternoon mêlée, sweating, smoking and looking around her, all she could see was a mass of dark faces, none of which held any meaning for her. A few mildly interested people glanced at Gina as they went about their daily business, but of course there was no familiar face to make her feel wanted, not even a smile from some friendly stranger. Her shirt was starting to stick uncomfortably to her back. She threw her spent cigarette-end down and twisted it out beneath her sandaled foot. She thought briefly of Richard but couldn't summon the energy to feel guilty about her brief fantasy. She started to walk along the pot-holed street.

As Gina wandered slowly and randomly through the streets she thought about the tiger sanctuary and wondered if it were worth trying to get there. She thought vaguely about going to the bus station to find out which bus to take, but knew that the chaos and commotion she would find there would make her feel dizzy; better to go later or maybe tomorrow. Gina kept walking, not at all sure where she was going, allowing herself to be bumped and jostled along by the busy people hurrying around her. How on earth were there so many rushing people in this small town, she thought tetchily; where could they all be going? Gina tripped, grazing the side of her foot on the uneven road-surface, swore to herself inaudibly and stumbled on.

A moped supporting three people and a huge bag of something sped past too close to her, hooting, and someone shouted. Was he shouting at her? Gina looked around and jumped back quickly as more mopeds zoomed past, some of them carrying impossible loads, one of them carrying something that resembled a fridge. Gina stumbled into a young Indian man wearing jeans, good shoes and white shirtsleeves, carrying a briefcase and talking loudly in Tamil into a mobile phone. He raised his arms at his sides in a gesture of frustration as Gina mumbled an embarrassed apology. Someone was laughing and Gina turned, feeling disorientated and bewildered. There seemed to be people and mopeds rushing everywhere, and Gina felt herself sweating and swaying in the rising heat and confusion. She ploughed on and pushed through a group of ragged, giggling youths who were taunting a skinny dog with a stick, past some leathery, chattering old men wearing faded white Punjabi pyjamas, drinking chai outside a ramshackle café, two fat women in saris and lots of gold jewellery debating loudly and animatedly in a shop doorway. A bewildered-looking old man wearing a dirty, ragged kurta, who appeared to have only one arm, lurched towards Gina saying something in a garbled voice. He stared into her face, his eyes rheumy, his open mouth revealing an incomplete set of uneven black teeth. Gina looked around, her eyes wide with alarm, but the man shuffled past her, mumbling to himself. Faces began to merge, a cacophony of chattering, shouting, laughter, of people, dogs, mopeds.

I need to sit down, Gina thought. She swayed to a nearby café, which had an open front and a few rickety metal chairs and tables outside and flopped down on a seat, partly shaded by a ragged white canopy, relieved to be out of the bustle and the rush of the street. She was thankful that there was a small tin ashtray on the table in front of her. It was twisted and bent and she noticed absently that it had a picture of a blue tiger inside it, partially obscured by cigarette ends, one of which was still smoking faintly. As she looked around her, Gina noticed that the other customers were all men, middle aged or old, wearing white pyjamas, and engaged in earnest conversations. One or two glanced at her curiously but went back to their discussions. It appeared that a lone white woman was not cause for much comment here. Gina was glad. When at last a skinny young serving-man came and lifted a desultory eyebrow at her, she asked for a coffee and a bottle of water before taking her pack of cigarettes and her lighter gratefully out of her pitifully cheery bag.

While she was waiting for her drinks, Gina smoked slowly, drawing comfort from the familiar soothing effect of the ritual. She put the cigarette to her mouth, caressing it with her lips, savouring its acrid taste, its damp solidity, drawing deep into her throat the sweetly corrupting smoke, holding it there for as long as she could before gradually exhaling a languid coil of smoke which snaked away from her. She felt numbed. She told herself that she wasn't used to the heat, wasn't used to the crowds.

Gina leaned back in her chair, righting herself as it wobbled to one side, one of its legs shorter than the others. She was in a busy street, lined with dilapidated shops and grimy-looking cafés. This was not an area for tourists and had none of the statues of gods and goddesses or the cheap western clothes and imitation designer handbags that the shacks which lined the streets near their hotel specialised in. Instead, Gina took in the strange-looking fruits and flowers, fiercely coloured spices, haphazard piles of random hardware, vibrantly dyed sari material. There was a pavement of sorts on one side of the road, but the surfaces of both were potholed and uneven, and the pavement disappeared altogether in places. There were piles of stinking rubbish at intervals along the roadside. In the gutter wiry dogs sniffed and pawed listlessly among rotting fruit and unidentifiable debris, or sprawled out, sleeping in the shade with no heed for the passersby who stepped over their supine forms.

As she sat there taking in the scene, she caught whiffs of the stench of the rubbish, acrid and sour, mixed with the fragrance of exotic incense from some nearby temple. Faint sounds of chanting came now and then through the chatter and hum of the busy street. Toward the far end of the road, Gina could see a bony, hump-backed cow slumped near the side of the road, people and vehicles ignoring its dusty bulk, skirting around it, unperturbed by its obstruction. Everything seemed to be happening either at twice the usual speed, the kamikaze traffic, the rushing people, or, like the cow and the dogs, at a languid and indolent pace. Gina felt some empathy with the cow. The sun was bright with a metallic vividness that brought everything around her into sharp, almost violent relief; the heat was a force as solid as a block of angry colour.

A young woman in a pretty orange-and-red sari ripped through Gina's reverie. She was holding a big, misshapen basket, and was carrying a tiny baby on her front in a bright-yellow sling. The woman was crossing the road, and as she looked around to check for traffic, her long, glossy-black plait flicked from one side to the other before settling again down her back. Gina stared at her and the world slowed down. As the woman came closer, Gina could see the baby's face, the dark, creamy velvet skin, its perfect downy cheeks. Everything else disappeared, and as she looked into the infant's black eyes, she knew that it was a baby boy. He looked as though he had been nestled against his mother's breast since the dawn of time, resolute, indestructible, an inseparable part of the mother. The baby was tiny and he looked fragile and vulnerable, lying there helplessly dependent, trusting that his mother would care for him, love him, keep him safe. Gina looked at the mother. She looked serene, as though nothing and no one could rock this unassailable world of two. Her free hand rested lightly on the baby's back through the cotton sling, and Gina imagined that this comforted them both, reassured them of their symbiotic existence. The woman's silver bangles glinted in the sun as she stopped and seemed to consider something for a moment. She had crossed the road and stood by Gina's table. Gina sat very still. The mother hoisted her baby slightly and began rummaging in her basket. The baby made a small hiccupping sound followed by a gurgle, a sound so pure it cleansed the air, and Gina watched as the mother looked at her baby, an expression of intimate tenderness, a smile that made her features utterly divine.

Gina jerked, suddenly aware of a serving man with a thin face and grubby white apron standing by her table looking worried. He was saying something to her. Her drinks were on the table in front of her and Gina felt momentarily confused. 'You okay, miss? You okay?'

Gina realised with horror that she was crying – her face was wet, her shoulders hunched, her cigarette burned away to nothing between her fingers. One or two of the other tables' occupants were looking enquiringly in her direction. Gina hurriedly squashed the cigarette-end into the blue-tiger ashtray and wiped her face with the back of her hand. Her throat ached and she was afraid to speak in case her voice cracked, but she nodded to the waiter and made herself busy opening the top of her water bottle. The waiter looked relieved and turned to go back into the café, and Gina had a fleeting image of herself as he must see her, a strange white woman alone, crying at a table. She sniffed, wiped her face with her hand again and tried to compose herself. She took two, three gulps of her water. It was warm but she felt grateful for it all the same. As she placed the plastic bottle down and picked up the chipped white mug of lukewarm coffee, Gina looked up. The woman and baby were gone. Gina put her hand to her stomach and let it rest there, gently. She stared ahead of her, and this time the tears were hot and silent and she let them fall.

Chapter 22 – Sandrine

19th December 1967

My Perelle,
I have spent a lot of time with the yogi. He has told me
some amazing things. I have decided to stay for a while.
He told me that for all my travelling I am not free. He
said I am in my 'Prabrajya', my period of wandering. I
was intrigued. He told me about a legend, the legend of
the great virgin goddess Kumari who single-handedly
conquered the demons and secured freedom for the
world. He asked me what the legend said to me. I said I
didn't know, but perhaps we all have demons to
conquer. Perelle, something in that old man's words has
touched me. I feel that perhaps I have something to
learn from him. When I went back there with a bag full
of mangoes, he smiled at me and the corners of his
eyes crinkled like yours. Something he said comes back
to me night after night. He told me to imagine Papa as a
five-year-old child. I imagine him on a dark hillside,
looking up into a clear night sky, wonder in his wide
eyes, marvelling at the vast firmament above and
whispering theories about what the stars could be.
Perelle, something in this vision makes me cry a little
and there is something strange in my tears, something
that makes me want to speak further with this yogi.

Chapter 23 – Rachel

'Why didn't Gina want to come to Mumbai with you?'

The question was posed innocently as Pravi raised an inquisitive eyebrow and sipped his cappuccino. His elbows were on the table in front of him, his shoulders slightly hunched.

Rachel was surprised by the question. She frowned slightly. 'Well, we did talk about it before we came to India. We had planned to come here together, but I think when the time came, she thought it was too far to go.'

'But you said you'd travelled quite a lot together before?' His voice was soft, his diction precise.

Rachel looked at her chai and shifted slightly in her seat. 'Yes we had, but somehow it was different before – maybe because we don't usually have a permanent base as we do here. We are more used to moving around a lot. Perhaps she just wanted to stay in one place for a change.'

Rachel felt defensive. This explanation sounded superficial and hollow. She clasped her hands around her mug, enjoying the comforting feel of the heat.

'Are you sure that's the reason?' Pravi's question was gentle.

'Well, no, not really.'

They were sitting in a coffee shop in the centre of Mumbai, waiting for Vish, with whom they would be staying. The café was part of a chain – 'Coffee Day' – and the stark, neon brightness of the modern interior contrasted baldly with the darkness of the street outside. Rachel had been surprised that such domestic franchises existed in India, and immediately felt annoyed with herself, not wanting to be in any way condescending. The coffee shop could have been anywhere in the consumerist west. Its clean, straight lines, tiled flooring, air-conditioning and generic coffees spoke of London, Paris, New York. There was a sense in which Rachel was relieved that she didn't have to worry about possible unclean conditions and the diseases associated with them as she did in some local cafés. But she didn't warm to the standardised sophistication of Coffee Day and she felt faintly marginalised, alienated even, by its bland generality.

They were the only customers here. Pravi leant back in his plastic chair, his legs stretched out to the side of the table. He yawned widely and stretched his head from left to right as though trying to relieve stiffness. 'Perhaps your friend is not feeling as adventurous as she usually does?'

'Well perhaps,' Rachel mumbled, stretching out her own legs under the table.

Pravi spoke quietly. 'She seems pre-occupied, somewhere else – like something is bothering her.'

Rachel felt uncomfortable, not liking where this probing appeared to be going. Pravi's questioning was friendly, enquiring, not at all accusing, but even so Rachel felt a creeping intensity.

'What makes you think something is bothering her?' She asked the question lightly, trying to keep the conversation congenial.

Pravi's answer, though, was too close to Rachel's own feelings of uneasiness about Gina. 'She seems distracted, not focused on now. She is not at peace. That night on the beach – what was she crying about?'

Rachel looked up. 'Well to be honest,' she answered, putting her chai down, 'I thought it was the alcohol – she had drunk far too much.' Her answer didn't sound very honest.

'She was sad,' Pravi countered simply. His voice was mild but somehow contained a heavy sense of import.

Pravi had made an interesting observation, though. Rachel had been focused on Gina's distress after she and Pravi had come back from along the beach. She hadn't really considered the fact that Gina had been upset before she and Pravi went for their walk. Once again, Rachel thought about the fact that she hadn't talked with Gina about it, hadn't asked Gina what was really troubling her.

Early on in their trip, they had gone to buy Indian SIM cards so that, should they need to, they could call home or each other cheaply without having to find a call-box. They did this whenever they travelled, so that if they ever got into any trouble they could always contact someone. Once they had their local SIM cards, Rachel had called her parents to let them know that she had arrived and was safe. She had been surprised when Gina had said that she didn't want to call Richard as she always did at the start of any of their trips.

'Won't he be worried if he doesn't hear from you?' Rachel had asked.

'I'll email him,' Gina had replied, something sharply metallic in her voice that Rachel couldn't place. Rachel had asked once more, a few days later, whether Gina had spoken with Richard yet. They hadn't been to an internet café, so Rachel knew that Gina hadn't had the opportunity to email him.

'Look, can you just leave it?' Gina had snapped. 'I'll call him when I'm ready.' Rachel had felt surprised by this, but hadn't questioned Gina and after a while had forgotten about it. She now began to wonder whether something was wrong with Gina that had nothing to do with anything that had happened in India.

Rachel took a deep breath and picked up her mug of chai. She stared into it as though some answer to the mystery of Gina's state of mind might be lurking there. She looked up at Pravi. 'Do you think I am shallow?'

Her question felt like a brave one – she was afraid of what the answer might be and she knew that Pravi would be honest with her. She wanted some reassurance that she hadn't acted selfishly in leaving Gina behind.

Pravi's answer wasn't encouraging, but was straight, and it pricked her like a blade. 'Shallow, no,' he said. 'Self-centred, yes.'

Pravi seemed to warm to this turn of conversation. 'Okay,' he said, leaning forward in his chair, 'I will tell you what I think.'

He looked out of the window and appeared to be considering his response. He always seemed to think carefully before he spoke, and Rachel had thought that this was to get his English right. Now though, she could see that it wasn't just that. He wanted his responses to be measured, precise. Rachel supposed that this was a good thing, if slightly wearing.

Rachel followed Pravi's gaze as he considered his answer to a group of five or six bare-footed and ragged street-children. They were small and thin and looked about seven-years-old. They were playing together, running around each other by the roadside, laughing loudly and pushing one another in a good-natured, teasing way. All the same, Rachel saw something feral, fearful in their eyes. There was something tense, something watchful, in the way that these children related to one another, to their surroundings. These were children who had learned how to protect themselves. Rachel heard an angry shout, and the children reacted at once, tearing down the dark street on their skinny legs and bare feet as a fat policeman started out after them from across the road. One of the children tripped and fell, and as he was staggering to his feet, the puffing policeman caught hold of the boy's arm. Rachel watched aghast as the man brought out a thin, truncheon-like weapon and started to beat the child around the back and arms. The child writhed, his face contorted into an ugly mask of pain before managing to wriggle free and run after his friends who were nowhere to be seen. Rachel stared open-mouthed at Pravi who was watching the policeman walk back across the road with a look of apparent passivity. 'Street children have a hard life here,' was all he said.

Pravi looked back squarely at Rachel and spoke to her in a low, even voice, articulating each word carefully. 'Rachel, you wouldn't be as adventurous as you are if you were any less self-centred. You yearn for new experiences, and you seem to place these above all else.' He looked intently at Rachel before continuing. 'I think you connect deeply with your experiences. I think you also connect deeply with people, but you leave them behind in the same way you leave the places you visit behind.'

Rachel stared at him, trying to focus on his words. She could see how he might think this of her, considering their own relationship. But she wasn't sure she agreed with him. It was clear to her that he was alluding to her friendship with Gina, and she paused before answering, trying to get her thoughts into some kind of coherent order.

'But I've known Gina for years,' she said eventually. 'We are close friends; we are comfortable with each other. We can tolerate disagreements. It won't harm our friendship that I came to Mumbai without her.'

Rachel had known that Pravi would answer her honestly, but now she felt that she had to defend herself. But she somehow couldn't get the thread of what she felt threatened by, was it what Pravi was saying or what the policeman had done to the little boy?

'Well that's good,' Pravi answered, smiling. 'I haven't known you for long. All I can tell you is what I see, what I feel. I may be wrong.'

Rachel and Gina had met when they had both been accepted onto a graduate trainee programme at a publishing house. Amid the busy hush of their open-plan office they had discovered a mutual appreciation of long lunches, after-work cocktails, travel books and foreign films. Sharing these passions had enabled them to find a way into their new professional world and to make the transition from their former scholarly idealism to a new, more pragmatic existence. They laughed together, planned together and eventually travelled together. After a time Rachel had joined the marketing team and Gina had secured an editorial position with a bigger publishing house. The two had gone on to spend many a happy, usually inebriated hour or two planning their many trips together.

But as time and careers continued to hijack them, Gina had moved from her rented flat to an inevitably heavily mortgaged one closer to her office. She had begun to see a lot of one of the development editors at her company, and eventually they became a couple – engaged since last year. Meanwhile, Rachel now worked longer hours at her own office. She was hoping to secure a post as a brand manager before very long. They were both busy creating the conventionality of career and domestic trappings and less often than they used to found the time to spend evenings dreaming and planning adventures.

Even so, Rachel considered her relationship with Gina to be a good friendship. She thought about Pravi's words: that she didn't connect deeply with people. She knew Gina's past, had listened to her stories, knew her family. She said as much to Pravi.

'But does Gina know yours?' he replied.

Rachel felt suddenly irritated that this stranger could attempt to sum up her character within days of meeting her. 'But I am a good listener – everyone says so.'

'Yes, I think you are, but do you think you deny others the opportunity to listen? Do you give?'

Years before, Rachel's only long-term, serious relationship had ended abruptly just after they had both graduated. He had apparently decided that variety was worth more than fidelity and had left Rachel to pursue a life of licentious bachelorhood. For days she didn't go out, didn't get dressed, didn't eat properly. Alone in her room she wept and slept and played through in her mind the thousand ways she could have pre-empted this, saved the relationship, stopped him from leaving her. But throughout her grieving the loss of her relationship, she didn't tell anyone any of her feelings, not even her parents with whom she was living at the time. Of course she told her family, her friends the fact that her relationship had ended. But Rachel kept her feelings to herself and only re-engaged with the world once she felt that she had them sufficiently under her control. Rachel knew that her parents felt relieved that she had dealt with this unpleasant situation in this way, and she endeavoured to carry on with her life with as much normality as possible. Eventually Rachel felt herself able to relegate her despair to some rarely visited part of her inner world. She emerged, butterfly-like, and continued with her life.

Rachel told this story to Pravi as an illustration of her view that she was not self-centred. She was surprised by his response.

'In that time,' Pravi replied, 'what were you centred on?'

'Well, of course on myself,' she answered, 'but what I meant was, I didn't impose that on others – that's the point.'

Pravi looked at her steadily and drained the last of his coffee before he replied. 'I think your self-centeredness separates you from others,' he said slowly.

'You mean I run away from intimacy.' It was a statement rather than a question.

'You don't connect with people deeply for long. You leave them behind.'

Chapter 24 – Gina

'Thank you so much, I'm fine.' Gina was unsure how long she'd been at the café. She'd paid for her drinks and the curious men had lost interest in her, so she had been quietly sitting there for some time. She couldn't make her thoughts make sense. Her tears had stopped but she felt as though she were in a landscape devoid of significance. As she looked about her and stared at the objects all around, they seemed to fix with meaningless audacity to her vision, bewildering her, taunting her. She knew their names – 'bike', 'man', 'cow', 'chair' – but the names had become mere verbal abstractions and somehow no longer bore any relationship to the things themselves. People walked past with no more meaning than this chair, that ashtray, that damned stupid, bent-tin ashtray with its outrageous blue tiger. What did it mean, she thought. What could it possibly mean for her? She stared perversely at the tiger hiding beneath the cigarette ash and stubs and tried to will it to provide for her some kind of an anchor, a foothold to something solid, tangible, something authentic.

She didn't know what to do. She wanted to find something, someone that would ground her, guide her, steer her back towards the certain world. She looked around her, stared at everything, everyone. I don't know how to be here, she thought. I don't know how to be.

Some part of Gina watched herself. 'Come on Gina,' she heard it say as she stood up, gathered her things together into the red bag and walked steadily away from the café, placing one foot resolutely in front of the other, keeping her eyes forward, avoiding the people she passed, and not thinking. 'Come on Gina.' All she was aware of was her own forward momentum and the obstacles in front of her, which had to be avoided. She circumnavigated people, dogs, cows, traffic, managed to make her way along the maze of roads and alleyways to the bus station and the taxi rank nearby, where she spoke slowly to the driver, negotiating the fare to her hotel. Her own voice sounded as distant to her as the traffic and cows. 'That's it. Come on.' Gina sat in the back of the cab not thinking, not speaking until they arrived thirty minutes later at the hotel. She took her purse from her bag, paid the fare and thanked the driver. She nodded at the security guard at the front of the hotel and found her way to the room, where she let herself in and locked the door behind her. Then this watching-Gina made her walk to the bedroom, lie down on the bed and sleep.

Chapter 25 – Sandrine

27th January 1968

My dear Perelle,

I send you these letters without knowing if you receive them. Without response, I have the freedom to continue on my own path. It seems to me that I am using you as my fixed point, my pole star. You are perhaps the paper I write on. You give my words somewhere to land, sanctuary to the butterflies in my heart. You told me once that all that we do we do for ourselves, do you remember? Even acts of altruism, you said, were to satisfy a need. I believed you. And so I have told myself now that in your absence all I need is your name, your shade, the idea of you. I tell myself that it is enough. I told you a long time ago that I learned something from you about honesty. About authenticity and integrity. Do you remember me telling you, Perelle? We were staying at that beautiful hotel on the hill that time we went to Strasburg. Papa had gone out with friends and we were to stay at the hotel. I came to your room. We sat on your balcony looking down at the town and we talked about freedom. You said that you wanted to be a bird, you wanted to fly. You seemed angry and sad and you talked for a long time about flying away. Do you still want to fly, Perelle?

I am staying with the yogi now. I have a tiny room that is not much more than a cell, but it is sufficient for my needs. Each morning we perform asanas and we meditate. He tells me to say a word, 'Om', over and again in my mind. I find a kind of peace there,

Sometimes the yogi talks to me and sometimes he doesn't. He says that I must look within and that this word 'Om' will help me to do that.

I find that I think a lot about you here where it is quiet and peaceful and away from the bustle of the town. I have realised that you gave me more than your time and that I continue to take from you. You still move me, Perelle. We had a language once. What we gave to one another we knew was received. You said that I don't judge you. You said that because of this you could tell me anything. It is true, and this is why I continue to write to you, to give you my words. Although these letters sail off alone, I know that you will read them, somehow, somewhere. Maybe sitting in our old café in the Rue de Valence, drinking your black coffee and smoking. I can see you there now, cigarette smoke making your features vague, old Broteaudeau limping behind you with his tray and his cloth askance over his bent shoulder. Or perhaps you will unfold my letter in your apartment before beginning your day. Perhaps in your bed. Your fingers will touch this paper, these very words. They will enter you as you rise from sleep, muzzy and soft among the sheets. Perhaps they will move you, Perelle, as your words moved me all that time ago.

Chapter 26 – Rachel

Vish was a lean young man, wiry and sinewy, and he looked to be in his late twenties. He and Pravi had greeted each other warmly, hugging and clasping one another's shoulders. There was much head wobbling in that uniquely Asian way that Rachel liked to observe. Vish had looked at Rachel through narrowed eyes and had greeted her politely, if somewhat coolly. Beyond a few courteous pleasantries about their journey, he didn't speak much to her. Instead he and Pravi chatted easily together, enquiring after each other's friends and family. They spoke in English, and Rachel wondered what language they would use if she were not there. Although Rachel didn't feel part of their rapport, she did feel privileged to witness it. Vish and Pravi had never met before. Vish was a friend of one of Pravi's friends, and the plan was to stay at his aunt and uncle's apartment in Goregaon to the north of the city. Rachel considered this a much better idea than staying in a hotel. She was looking forward to meeting the family and staying at their home. And she didn't mind that Vish appeared cool towards her. They were, after all, strangers to one another.

It appeared to Rachel that the rules of their opening dialogue involved exchanging information about family members. Pravi spoke about his grandfather who had been a shop-keeper in Mumbai, and in turn Vish told Pravi about his own grandfather. Rachel was fascinated, not only by what they were saying, but also by the way their words created an immediate connection and intimacy with one another. They spoke respectfully, gently and appreciatively of one another's backgrounds. Rachel thought about how different their conversation was from that of two western men meeting for the first time. By the time they arrived at Vish's uncle's apartment, Rachel thought that they probably already knew more about one another than she and Gina knew about each other.

When they arrived at the apartment it was already late at night and although tired, Rachel felt exhilarated by the hour-long local train-ride on the Mumbai Western Line. They'd got on at Mumbai Central, having walked the fifteen or so minutes from the café through Mumbai's dark but lively streets. Although it was late, there were plenty of people about, standing around in groups or hurrying on their way. They passed a van where a group of five or six policemen were lounging, some leaning against the van, some sitting in the open back. Rachel supposed their sand-coloured uniforms and their smart blue hats were meant to be reassuring to someone such as herself, but she wasn't so sure as she thought about the policeman who had beaten the boy. They climbed some steps to cross a road bridge near the station, and in the darkness Rachel noticed piles of black binbags full of stinking rubbish lying all along the stairs and the back wall of the bridge. Her stomach lurched when she noticed movement, and it dawned on her with a reluctant comprehension that these weren't binbags at all; they were people huddling together, sleeping on the bridge. Rachel stared at them and hurried close to Pravi and Vish.

At Mumbai Central Vish bought their tickets from an ill-tempered-looking man behind a dirty glass window. He had looked at Rachel with an expression of frowning doubt on his face, as though he didn't quite believe what Vish was asking for. They had a short wait for the train on the crowded platform where they attracted occasional looks from the skinny, scruffy men around them, who were standing, sitting and lying in every available space. Rachel couldn't tell by looking at them which of these men were homeless and trying to find some miserable shelter on the platform and which were waiting for a train.

When the huge and screeching train arrived and shrieked and juddered its way to a halt, Rachel stayed as close to Pravi and Vish as she could and crammed with a great mass of others into a dimly lit carriage that was already heaving with passengers. She watched with incredulity as those who weren't lucky enough to squeeze inside the train clung on outside the carriage. As they stood, jammed against countless other sweating and swaying passengers, hanging onto a dirty leather roof-strap for support, Rachel realised that, as far as she could tell, not only was she the sole female in their carriage, she was the only westerner. Curious locals stared at her with a complete lack of inhibition, but Pravi and Vish's presence reassured Rachel and she didn't feel self-conscious or threatened. She accepted the curiosity of the men around her as readily as she noted her own curiosity about them. Indeed, she felt that she had the better deal, there was far more for her to be curious about.

The carriage became steadily less crowded as the train lurched to a stop at intermittent local stations. Rachel watched the names come and go in eager silence: Borivali, Bhavander, Vasai Road. Each name reflected and reinforced Rachel's sense of difference and otherness as she tried to burn the words into her memory by repeating them over again in her mind.

When she was able to see out of the dirty window, she saw that the train was clattering slowly past the inevitable railway slums. It was dark and she couldn't see much but could tell from the shapes, the fires and the occasional glimpse into the meagre dwellings that people, families were making a life here. She thought of them sleeping in those flimsy wooden structures, rags for blankets, and wondered what they were dreaming of.

They eventually reached Goregaon, where they alighted along with the few others who were left on the train. Rachel wondered who these men were, where were they coming from and going to, so late at night. Once again she hurried after Vish and Pravi – no one seemed to walk slowly in Mumbai – as they made their way over a footbridge to where some auto-rickshaws were waiting. They passed small groups of hostile-looking young men, standing around smoking and talking quietly, and others lying asleep in any space they could find – on a car bonnet, in a gutter, against the station wall. Rachel felt immeasurably glad that she wasn't alone, and she followed closely behind Pravi and Vish into a waiting auto-rickshaw. The ride took another fifteen minutes or so, bumping along dark, potholed roads lined with rubbish and gloomy buildings, where painfully thin dogs seemed to roam in packs, ever watchful, always moving. They came into a district full of big square blocks of flats. Here, sleeping security-guards manned huts at the gated entrances to the buildings, and Rachel supposed that this was where Mumbai's middle class lived. After stopping at one such apartment building and bundling out of the auto-rickshaw, Vish paid the driver, walked over to the hut and woke the fat guard. Rachel and Pravi followed, hoisting their backpacks, and waited while Vish said

something to the guard in what Rachel supposed was
Marathi. The guard glanced at Rachel with what looked
to her like scorn and snorted before rolling his yellowy
eyes and grinning, showing gappy, even yellower teeth.
Rachel looked at Vish who was opening the block door
with his key and wondered what he had told the guard.
Vish had still not spoken to her beyond the introductory
pleasantries, and she began to wonder whether his cool
attitude towards her was in fact hostility rather than
shyness as she had at first supposed. She felt like a waif
as she trailed after the two men, up concrete flights of
stairs onto a dark, severe landing and waited whilst Vish
fumbled with his keys again and let them into the
apartment.

The door opened onto what Rachel first thought was
a large, dark vestibule but quickly realised was in fact a
small room. It was furnished with a few wooden chairs
(one rather surprisingly painted blue) and a small
wooden chest. Beyond this Rachel could see a tiny
kitchen, which opened onto another dark room at the
back of the flat. Rachel supposed it must be a bedroom
but changed her mind when, having taken off their
sandals at the front door, she and Pravi were shown
through. There was a large wide wooden couch in this
room, another small chest and some floor cushions.
Rachel took off her backpack and looked around her.
She sat down on the couch. It was very hard. There was
no carpet anywhere and the floors seemed in an unlikely
way to be made of marble. There was no light inside the
flat (although there appeared to be light fittings), and
the only thing lighting the place was the not-quite-full
moon shining bleakly through the large window at the
back of the room. This created a gloomy glow which

cast dark shadows around the furniture and into the corners of the room.

Rachel and Pravi sat on the couch in the semi-darkness and glanced at one another. Pravi smiled and cocked one eyebrow. They could hear a conversation taking place in another room, two male voices, one of them Vish's. As they listened, the dialogue began to sound insistent, and as the voices became louder and continued for some time, Rachel felt a growing unease.

Eventually a large, balding, middle-aged man wearing white Punjabi pyjamas entered the room with Vish behind him. Both were frowning. Vish announced that this was his uncle. Rachel and Pravi got up quickly, Rachel saying hello and Pravi saying something in Hindi, their words stumbling into each other's clumsily. Rachel held out her hand. The man glowered as he took it for the briefest of seconds and met her eye only fleetingly. He appeared to be very tense, shifting his weight from one bare foot to the other. He evidently spoke no English and appeared at a loss to know how to deal with Rachel. Instead he said something to Pravi, his voice low, clipped. Pravi appeared chastened and looked down at his feet. Everyone was silent for a moment until Vish indicated to Pravi that he should follow him into the other room. Rachel was left alone with the older man and, not knowing how she should behave, smiled hesitantly. The man stared at her coldly for a long second, shook his head slowly and turned to leave the room.

Rachel sat back down on the couch. She folded her arms in front of her, feeling tense. Pravi came back in, no longer smiling, with Vish behind him.

'Rachel,' he said, 'we have a difficult situation here.' He frowned and pursed his lips, appearing to look for the right words.

'It appears that Vish's aunt has been called away – her daughter is having a baby and she will not return for some days. There is no woman here.'

Rachel felt perplexed. She looked enquiringly from Pravi to Vish and back to Pravi.

'I am not sure if you understand the cultural significance of this situation,' Vish said, 'but your being here puts us all in a very difficult position.'

Rachel was worried. The cultural complexity of the situation was not lost on her, but she felt at a loss to know what she could do to rescue it. And more to the point, she thought, was she to spend the night in a flat in a strange city with three men she didn't know? She briefly wondered if they had tricked her, if the aunt perhaps didn't exist at all. Indeed, she thought, the place looked barely inhabited with its sparse furnishings and lack of adornment. She saw no evidence of a woman living here. But no, that's silly, she told herself. The uncle's hostility and discomfort supported the explanation that Vish had given, and Pravi looked uncertain as well. Vish's dark expression seemed to suggest that she was somehow responsible for the position he found himself in.

'Well, I'm very sorry,' she said falteringly, 'but what can we do?'

Vish sneered at her as though she were the most stupid woman he had met. She suddenly wondered if they meant to throw her out, which would surely be worse than having to stay here with the men. Rachel's mind flashed back to the men standing around by the station and to the roaming packs of dogs.

'Well it's too late to arrange anything else.' There was something nasty in his voice as Vish replied, 'You will have to stay with us.'

Chapter 27 – Sandrine

2nd March 1968

My darling brother,
Meditation is difficult. My mind won't stay still but instead flits between memories, plans and fantasies. I must use greater strength and discipline to bring it back to the still and silent centre. The yogi says that fasting will help, and so today I fast. It is mid-morning and so far my body feels good. He told me to be aware of my thoughts because thoughts have direction. He said that, from a thought, energy begins to emanate like ripples from a stone thrown into water. Thoughts can be born into the material world – they have their own power and energy. I think that perhaps I think too much of you, Perelle. I asked this of the yogi. He asked me if you free me or if you tether me. It was a good question. The answer is not so easy. I think maybe both.

Chapter 28 – Rachel

Rachel looked from Pravi to Vish and back to Pravi. Vish's eyes were narrow and there was something like a leer playing around his lips. Vish looked at Pravi and Rachel thought she caught the slightest flicker of complicity between them. Her heart was beginning to race.

'What's the matter Rachel?' Pravi said quietly. 'Sit down.'

Rachel sat.

'You look worried,' he said, speaking the words slowly and deliberately. 'What's the matter?'

'Well,' she whispered, 'Vish's uncle doesn't seem too happy for me to be here.'

'Don't worry about him.' He looked at Rachel intently. 'We will look after you.' His mouth was smiling but his eyes were not. 'Won't we, Vish?'

Rachel's common sense had somehow turned to a butterfly thing, and it danced dangerously from one construct to another fuelled by her exhaustion and disorientation. She must act normally, she told herself, not show her anxiety.

'Do you think,' she said, 'that we could eat something?' She wasn't hungry, but she couldn't think of anything else to say.

'There is no food in the apartment; didn't you eat on the train?' There was scorn in Vish's voice.

'Yes we did,' Rachel replied as brightly as she could. 'It isn't a problem. Do you think I might shower? I feel rather dusty from the journey.' As soon as she said this she regretted it, wondering immediately about the wisdom of her request.

'Come with me,' Vish said as he got up and led her to the vestibule, where there were two doors. Rachel looked at Pravi, who nodded at her to follow Vish.

'Here is the shower room.' He pushed open one of the doors. And here is the toilet. He gestured at the other door. 'It is an Indian toilet,' he added pointedly. It sounded to Rachel like a challenge.

'That's fine,' she said. 'Would it be okay if I shower now?'

Rachel collected her backpack and after using the Indian toilet – a tiny room containing nothing but a floor-level ceramic hole, a bucket, a tap and a cup – she entered the shower room, which housed a small sink and a metal hose hanging out of the ceiling. The shower rose appeared to be missing. There was a lock on the door. Thank God, Rachel thought. She leaned her back against the door, trying to gather her thoughts, to stop them from scattering into dangerous territory. She closed her eyes and took a deep breath. Her back and shoulders were aching and she felt utterly drained. She clearly couldn't leave this late at night on her own with nowhere to go. Should she call Gina? But what could Gina do hundreds of miles away? She would have to stay here; there was no alternative that Rachel could think of. Maybe it would be fine, she reasoned. It was late, they were all tired and perhaps they would just go to bed. But where was she expected to sleep? Perhaps she shouldn't sleep? But Pravi is a nice person, she thought. Or is he? What did she know? Vish certainly didn't seem nice. And the uncle was clearly hostile. The possibilities baited her. Rachel ran her hand through her hair. What have I done, she thought? She looked around her and decided that she might as well shower.

Rachel was astonished to discover that the water was hot, and having rummaged in her backpack for what she needed and worked out a way to keep her things dry, she stood under the warm water, closed her eyes and tried to calm her thoughts. From door to door, the journey from Kanyakumari to Mumbai had taken more than two days. She was exhausted, and the warm water felt wonderful on her aching limbs as she relaxed under it, and she almost cried as she watched the grime of these days washing away down the small hole in the corner of the floor. She thought of the situation she now found herself in – showering under a pipe in a flat in Mumbai which appeared to have no beds, whilst contemplating a night with three male strangers! She snorted, a half laugh. Her situation was almost comical. Perhaps poetic justice had dealt her a hand. God, she thought, that's not funny.

After she had showered, Rachel fumbled again in her backpack for her blue travel-towel and dried herself off as best she could. She still felt damp as she pulled on an old pair of grey jogging-pants and a big grey tee-shirt. She hoped that she looked suitably androgynous. After brushing her wet hair and bundling all her things into her backpack, she took a deep breath, closed her eyes and stood by the door for a moment. Then she unlocked it, fixed her smile and went into the back room.

Vish and Pravi were sitting on the couch, and they stopped talking as soon as Rachel entered. Pravi smiled a slight smile and raised one suggestive eyebrow. 'You are ready for bed?'

'I am very tired,' replied Rachel carefully.

Pravi stood up. He hesitated by Rachel, looking down at her. He put his hand on her shoulder and Rachel fought not to flinch. Pravi laughed, shook his head and left the room. Rachel put her backpack into the corner of the room and turned around.

'Come,' said Vish, patting the couch, 'Sit.'

In the absence of any alternative Rachel sat down on the couch next to Vish. She pulled her knees up to her chin and hugged her legs. Vish nodded at her. She nodded back. After a while, Vish sighed as though he were giving in to an annoying child and said, 'So, it is your first time in Mumbai, I take it.'

It was a statement rather than a question and was the first full sentence that Vish had directed at her since they met at the café. Rachel told him that it was indeed her first time here.

'You need more time,' Vish said, his words dismissing her already. 'You don't have time to see all there is.' He was frowning slightly and sounded irritated.

'That's okay,' Rachel replied quietly. 'I'm not really bothered about seeing all the tourist attractions. I simply wanted to experience being here – the train trip, the people, the streets, the buildings.'

'Ah yes,' said Vish, with slightly more enthusiasm. 'We have some very beautiful architecture here.'

'Yes, I'm sure you do, but it isn't really the beautiful places that I want to see. I am more interested in the everyday places – the everyday lives of the people.'

Vish looked at her distrustfully. 'Well,' he said, hesitating. 'You should see our beautiful buildings. Bhuleshwar temple for example, and the university. There are so many, too many to name now. You will find them all and many more absolutely stunning. Yes, we certainly do have some very beautiful architecture, and not just the English-built buildings. Very fine Indian buildings too.'

Vish nodded more emphatically and Rachel nodded back, not wanting to anger him. Vish continued, his precise diction and careful annunciation slicing away at the space between them.

'Of course we have some impressive modern buildings as well. The Mumbai Stock Exchange, for example, and the Nehru Planetarium. And of course Film City. All the tourists like that place. Very modern, very amazing.'

Rachel got the impression that Vish was desperate to highlight Mumbai's grandeur, its achievements both historic and contemporary, and for her not to know its sordid, squalid underbelly. It seemed as though he wanted to hold out Mumbai as a majestic city, impressive and fashionable, one capable of competing with her western notions of what it was to be a grand and modern city. Somehow his eagerness made Vish seem vulnerable, and this gave Rachel a little confidence. She wanted to keep Vish talking, but she gave up trying to explain her reasons for coming here and instead asked Vish about his work. Vish told her that he had a university degree and worked in a stockbroker's office. Eventually he aimed to be a stockbroker. This surprised Rachel and she looked at him with renewed interest. Without pause, Vish proceeded to explain to Rachel all the reasons why an Indian degree was more academically rigorous than a British degree. Rachel felt disappointed and listened to him half-heartedly. Vish was tiring her with all his insistent posturing, and she felt that she didn't know enough about the subject to give an informed opinion. She suspected that Vish didn't either.

Rachel started when Pravi came back in. He too was wearing jogging pants and a tee-shirt, and his hair was wet and tousled. Rachel could see the contours of his upper body beneath the clinging black cotton of his damp shirt. Their eyes met. Rachel looked quickly away. Pravi raised his eyebrows and grinned widely, but didn't sit down.

'Okay Rachel,' he said, 'will you be alright in here? We three will sleep in the other room.'

Rachel's relief was palpable. Pravi shook his head almost imperceptibly.

After some brief discussion about what time they should get up in the morning, Pravi and Vish left to join the uncle in the other room. Rachel was left alone with the big hard couch. She stood up and looked around her. She considered trying to jam one of the chairs under the door-handle, but doubted that would work if someone were determined to get in. But she no longer thought that they might. Instead she took her backpack and dumped it in front of the door. At least this wouldn't look so stupid if there were nothing to fear, although what good it would do if there were she couldn't think.

She looked around once more. The paucity of the room made her a little sad, and she looked out of the window for inspiration. The sickly yellow moon, almost full, illuminated countless identical apartment buildings. The thought occurred to her that, if this were Europe, the roofs and the walls of the buildings would be covered with satellite dishes. She tried to see into some of the windows, but they all looked dark. The street below was deserted. A dog barked in the distance and made her jump.

Rachel sighed deeply and turned back to the room. She went to her backpack, knelt beside it on the hard floor and took out all the things she would need for the morning. She laid them neatly at the side of the room before turning around and facing the couch. She wondered what she would do if Pravi knocked quietly on the door and entered the room, his body damp from the shower, his hair wild and tousled, but quickly put the thought away, telling herself that her exhaustion was making her muddled. She opened the thin woollen blanket that had been left on the couch and climbed under it. She did the best she could to improvise a pillow and then lay on her side, trying to find a comfortable way to position herself. She thought of Gina alone in Kanyakumari and wished again that she had never left her.

Chapter 29 – Sandrine

10th April 1968

Dearest Perelle,

You told me once, on a journey somewhere, I can't remember where, that you are 'unfinished'. I was happy that you spoke like that to me, but I wondered if you thought you ever would be finished. I want ask you this now, Perelle. Are you a masterpiece in the making, a sculpture lurking in the wood? I told you then that I thought that you were messy and that I was messy too.

Perelle, I don't know if I am fooling myself here. Here, in the yogi's house, I tell myself stories of peace and rest and of independence, authenticity and freedom from attachments, and yet so often I think of you. It has been so long since I received word from you. A word from you would elate me. And so I am not free; I have learned this here. But I have not learned what you tried to teach me. I can see that I don't yet want to leave you, but I am beginning to see that I must. When I was travelling, every time I arrived at a place, another town, a city, I would check the Post Office. Sometimes there was a letter from you, more often there wasn't. And so I remained shackled, tethered to you. I feel my weakness. I know it. I look at it full in the face. I have no questions for it, no answers. I think that as long as I remain here with the yogi, you will begin to recede, to transform. Perhaps there will be a freedom in that, as he says. You are already becoming a muse, no longer a man. Perhaps I thought that I could write you away with my letters, perhaps write myself into the space that you occupy. I will mail this letter, and if after two months I don't hear from you, it will be my last. I have realised that you were right when you told me that 'I love you' means 'I want something from you'. My love for you seems to demand a response from you. You told me that if you could change anything in your life you would change our parents. Would you be 'finished' then, Perelle? Would I? We both ran away in our own different ways. We are alike, but I know we can't run together. I know this, but sometimes in the past, being with you has made me believe that I am free. If I were truly free, I would rip your address from my memory, burn it, throw the ashes into the wind to be carried far from me. Maybe, Perelle. But not yet. Write to me, my love. Give me your words. I will not write you again until you do. I am not yet free.

Chapter 30 – Gina

A small boy stands on a beach. He is a pale cream colour, pretty in that plump way that little boys are. His hair is brown. His curls blow long in the breeze. His shorts and tee-shirt are spattered with sand and are wet from playing in the sea. He is staring up the beach, towards a distant shack. The sun burns down; his skin may get burned. The tops of his bare feet and his freckly little snub-nose are already turning red in the hot sun.

The boy may be waiting for someone – or looking for them. He waits patiently. He may have been waiting for a long time. His hair continues to blow around his face. The boy doesn't brush it away. The sun beats down. Time passes.

A smile begins to play around the boy's lips. It isn't clear what he is smiling at. Even so the smile reaches his wide, dark eyes and they crinkle at the edges. Still he waits, and now he is less patient. He fidgets.

And there she is, at the far end of the beach, a spec, a dot, not much more yet but growing. The boy's smile widens as the figure draws closer. It becomes a grin and the child begins to hop, the way children do when they anticipate joy. She is coming.

She is coming. The figure doesn't rush, but walks along the beach at a steady pace. She looks straight ahead. Her bare feet leave a trail of prints behind her, and her skirt billows in the breeze. The boy looks as though he might rush to meet her, but he doesn't; he waits where he stands, but he starts to clap and laugh as little boys do when they are excited.

She is nearly here and the boy is jumping up and down in excitement.

'Mummy,' he shouts. It is a pure sound. 'Mummy, mummy!'

The woman is here. The little child is beside himself with joy. He hugs the woman tightly and looks up into her face. The woman looks down at the child. She looks up again and behind her at the footprints she has left and then forwards at the untouched sand ahead. She looks down at the little boy and takes his hand. He holds it tightly. She turns towards the sea.

The woman and the child walk hand-in-hand to the water's edge, towards the setting sun. The child looks up at his mother with trust in his brown eyes. The mother looks straight ahead. The waves rush back and forth tickling their toes. The child giggles with delight. The sunset is violent with its scarlet and crimson and citrus streaks. The sea is still warm. They keep walking.

They keep walking. The little boy looks again at the mother, but now there is a question in his wide eyes. The mother carries on walking straight ahead.

'Mummy?' the child says. The water is getting deep. The child is wading now; it isn't easy for him to walk as the water deepens. And now the water is up to his chest. Still the mother holds the child's hand and walks and stares ahead.

'Mummy!' The child is struggling now; his little feet can barely touch the seabed. He begins to kick his legs in an effort to stay upright. He loses his footing but can't struggle to the surface because the mother has hold of his hand. He splutters as he takes a gulp of sea water. His head goes under, once, twice, he swallows more water, he gulps the air when he can, but his little

123

face is beneath the sea now, he is thrashing around. The mother holds fast onto his hand...

How long have they been standing in the sea? The sun has almost set but still casts its death over the darkening water. It is cold now. The boy is still. His perfect little body is limp. His little fingers are flaccid but the mother continues to clutch them. Only now does she release them. The child's lovely hair streams around his face beneath the waves as he sinks. The woman looks straight into the cowardly sun until it shrinks to a hard black dot. She turns, walks out of the sea. She seems to hesitate for a moment at the water's edge, turns, looks back at the sea, turns again and continues her way up the beach onto the virgin sand.

Chapter 31 – Rachel

The child stared at her unwaveringly, its large brown eyes devoid of any emotion. It was standing no more than three feet away from her and holding out its little hand, palm upwards. She couldn't tell if it was a girl or a boy. She thought perhaps a boy – something in the high, pointed cheekbones, the skinny, knobbly legs streaked with dust. He wore a soiled and ragged tee-shirt and a pair of old grey shorts. He had no shoes on his filthy feet, and one bony foot was crossed over the other. The child, maybe three-years-old, stood completely still, silently imploring Rachel to place a coin into his hand. She didn't. She stared back at him and wondered about his life, his parents. Where had he slept last night? What had he eaten?

'Do you know what, Gina?' Rachel had said as they'd sat in her flat drinking hot chocolate and looking at a map of India. 'It says in the guide book that, since there is money in Mumbai, around three hundred people come here each day from rural villages hoping to make a better life for themselves and their families.' She'd looked up from her book. 'That's over two thousand people each week. It says here that as a consequence, six million people live in Mumbai's sprawling slums. Half the total population of the city.'

'Incredible,' Gina had replied. 'What a life.'

'But do you know what? They are not all beggars. It says here that the people who live in the slums do all the low-paying jobs that keep Mumbai going. Construction workers, train drivers, factory workers, the lot. And they are the lucky ones apparently. Some of them sleep on the streets and make a living by picking for glass, metal, cardboard, anything like that from, and I quote, "the stinking mounds of putrid waste in the municipal bins."' She had put the book down and looked up at Gina. 'Sounds like a great place to visit!'

Looking at the little boy, Rachel wondered sadly if this was the better life that his parents had expected to find when they bravely left their rural home. She thought of them in their distant village making their plans, talking to one another into the night about the opportunities that they would find in the city, how they would work hard to create a new home where they could raise their family, give their son a chance of a good life. She thought of them packing the few possessions that they would take with them. How frightened they must have been, leaving their family, their friends, their home, their way of life to make the long journey to the unknown city. Rachel looked at the child and wondered how this life could possibly be any better than the one left behind.

The little boy continued to stare with such hopeless conviction, lifeless sincerity and lack of awareness of anything other than Rachel that she almost laughed. He certainly wasn't the only beggar here – the busy station was a magnet for ruined and broken humanity of every kind and all around her she was aware of twisted and crippled old people, barely dressed children, men and women with matted hair and empty, staring eyes. But this child stood before Rachel, silently staring up at her, hand outstretched, as though this were all in his little life that he knew how to do.

Pravi had told her not to give money to beggars. 'Give food if you must, but do not give money.' Rachel had been prepared to cope with the beggars, to say no, to avoid eye contact, to keep walking. But she hadn't been prepared for the sheer numbers of the dispossessed that eked out an existence on Mumbai's streets. And this child had created such an intimacy with his proximity and steady eye-contact that Rachel felt she must do something for him in the face of such overwhelming wretchedness. She looked at Pravi, who was at the ticket desk talking to the clerk. She looked at the other waiting, jostling passengers. No one was taking the slightest notice of this tiny, hungry boy whose expectations for his life were nothing more than what his outstretched hand could receive. Rachel began to fumble in her backpack as Pravi turned and saw the child. He looked at Rachel.

'What are you doing?' he snapped. 'Rachel, there are a thousand like him. You can't give to them all. Besides, you give to one, they all come running. Come on.'

He pulled Rachel after him and led her through the ticket hall. Rachel thought about the apples in her backpack and imagined the boy staring after her, his little arm dropping to his side. She resisted the urge to look back at him.

'This is not your world, Rachel,' Pravi said, 'There are things you don't understand,'

Mumbai thrilled, frightened and disgusted Rachel. She was excited to be there but often felt like some kind of morbid voyeur, a poverty tourist. The beggars and the slum-dwellers attracted her gaze in a way that she found faintly repugnant, and she felt that she was using their wretched lives as some kind of sick local attraction. Often she felt overwhelmed. She wanted to be able to do something positive, make a difference, a contribution to the abject lives of these suffering people. But her feelings were vague and sentimental, and she hated herself at times for her middle-class sensibilities, reminding herself more than once that perhaps most of the world's people live like this. It was an impossible fact to digest, she thought, as behind Pravi's back she slipped an apple to an old woman with rheumy eyes and a bent and twisted arm.

But Rachel felt anger too. Not far from the sprawling rag-and-corrugated-plastic slum-cities were high-rise modern office-blocks and luxury shopping-malls where the affluent went to buy a place in the civilised world. She had seen this before on her travels, but not at such close quarters, and wondered not for the first time how the people and their governments could tolerate such extremes. Mumbai's slums were all the more incongruous because, as Vish had told her, the city was home to India's glamorous Bollywood film industry.

'More films are made here than in Hollywood,' he had said with pride.

'Yes,' Pravi had replied. 'Most of them about the lives of impossibly rich families who probably don't exist anywhere outside the Bollywood bubble.'

Rachel resigned herself to simply experiencing the many conflicting and contradictory faces of this extraordinary city.

They entered an air-conditioned, marble-floored mall and had a late breakfast of ragda patties and mango juice at a Jain café in the food hall, surrounded by large tropical plants in pots. Rachel wondered whether the Jain emphasis on vegetarian food which has caused no suffering might lessen the guilt she felt at being able to afford it. But as she looked around her she saw expensively clad young women with impossibly sleek hair and immaculate make up pushing plump and well-dressed babies in state-of-the-art pushchairs, dallying at shop windows full of sparkling gold, sumptuous material, works of art. Here and there at the food-hall tables were fashionable, well-groomed teenagers, chattering and giggling over their diet cokes. Pravi told her that Mumbai's young people often came to the cafés in the malls to escape the punishing heat outside. Rachel saw that some of these young women were wearing delicate, high-heeled sandals and pretty little ankle-chains. She thought about the old woman who had taken her apple and doubted that these young women had ever walked the potholed and shit-strewn streets where the slum-dwellers lived. She wondered whether the malls were an escape from more than just the heat. This was another Mumbai, and in a way it was just as shocking.

They had no plans and had spent much of the morning in Goregaon and on the western-line train with the commuters, the shoppers and the beggars. Rachel had woken to the sound of voices chatting and laughing. Vish had knocked on the door and peered around it tentatively. He brought her a cup of strong black coffee and somewhat surprisingly told Rachel that he had taken the morning off work to show her and Pravi around. They were waiting for her in the other room.

'No time to lose,' he said cheerfully. 'Plenty to see.'

Rachel told herself as she sipped the coffee that this proved how foolish she was capable of being when she was tired, and she vowed to make the most of her time in Mumbai and to start enjoying the trip again as she had before her exhausted state had played silly games with her mind.

Vish took them up the high, scrubby hill above the suburb to show them Film City far below in one direction and Mumbai itself in the other, the sparkling Arabian Sea sweeping away from the city in a wide arc. The three laughed easily together as they took photographs of each other with Vish's camera, and Rachel thought as she posed with Pravi for a picture, his arm flung carelessly over her shoulders, that after the complex and tacit drama of the night before, Vish definitely seemed to have thawed towards her.

Before lunchtime Vish left them at the station, and Rachel and Pravi took the train back to the centre of Mumbai. Rachel now saw the slums lining the railway track, which last night had been dark, almost homely shapes, for what they were – ramshackle, rickety constructions of wood, metal, plastic and rag. Alongside them and the railway line were huge hoardings advertising Bollywood films, the impossibly well-groomed and bejewelled actors mocking the meagre dwellings. Through the window Rachel caught glimpses of the little domesticity that must prevail wherever there are people. Clothes were being washed in a ditch beside the railway track, women were crouching to prepare meals over fires, and families were eating them in flapping-rag doorways, while children and old men squatted to relieve themselves by the railway line, staring at the trains as they passed.

Rachel texted Gina that morning – just a short message saying that they had arrived late last night and that she hoped that Gina was having fun. She hadn't heard back. She wondered why and whether she ought to phone. But no, she told herself that Gina was probably just busy getting on with her holiday. She would text back in her own good time. Rachel resolved not to think about Gina anymore. She could see no point in agonising over a situation over which she had no control. Pravi didn't mention Gina again either after his questioning at the café, and Rachel felt grateful for this.

They ate lunch at a busy Islamic café where harassed-looking Muslim men rushed around with steaming platefuls of Dahl and huge rotis.

'Is there anything you would like to do in particular this afternoon?' Pravi asked above the hubbub.

'Shall we just wander about?' Rachel answered. 'I'd really like just to be immersed in the place.'

So they spent the rest of the day negotiating the hot, frenetic streets. For most of the afternoon Rachel and Pravi said little to each other but walked at a steady pace in companionable silence, Rachel occasionally asking a question, Pravi answering in his quiet, unassuming way. The city seemed different in the daytime – less seedy. Fewer gangs of idle, loafing men lined the streets, and instead, people in Indian and western business-dress hurried through their day while vendors sold their wares from shops and shacks and stalls. But the poor of the city remained, and beggars of all ages made homes and beds of whatever they could find.

Late that afternoon Rachel told Pravi that she needed to relieve herself, and he pointed to a public toilet, a low, squat building with a light on inside. Rachel entered feeling a familiar apprehension about the conditions she might find. The sight that confronted her inside the building was more shocking than anything she had expected. Sitting on the floor of the toilet were around eight naked women covered in soap. In her embarrassment, Rachel wondered whether she should turn around quickly and leave, but the women were soaping themselves vigorously whilst chattering noisily to one another and took no notice of Rachel. She decided to carry on and went into a cubicle. When she came out the women were still washing, and she realised as she washed her own hands at a sink that they were laughing and talking as they removed the grime of the day in the only place they had access to running water. As she breathed the delicately perfumed soap, Rachel thought of the slum dwellings that were home to these proud women who were so diligently keeping themselves clean.

Rachel did indeed note some beautiful buildings. During the late afternoon they found themselves at the Gateway to India, and looking up at the ornately carved arch along with the other western tourists in their linen trousers and sun hats made her smile and think of Vish.

When evening came, Pravi said that they should make their way closer to the station and find a café where they could wait for their train. They hailed a taxi and got out close to the terminus where they found a café and ordered pomegranate juice.

'Lovely,' Rachel said to Pravi after taking a long gulp. 'But I am just so tired. I'm looking forward to being on the train.'

Chapter 32 – Sandrine

Today, after morning meditation, the words came and I felt so centred, so alive, so free. I felt them in my stomach, powerful and deeply coloured. I didn't even need to speak them, so strong was their power. Instead, I opened out with them and left myself for a little while. I tried to tell some of this to the yogi, but he raised his hand and closed his eyes. 'Keep your words close to your heart,' he said. 'They are just for you.'

Perelle, these things I tell you secretly, silently because I am telling myself. You are the keeper of my stories, the custodian. My words have found you, Perelle, even though I haven't spoken them, and although they are not for you, you have them. I watch myself here, sitting on the front step, looking up at the sky, closing my eyes, my head tilted upwards. The words are surging forward, and I love it that I can't stop them.

I will not mail this. I have not heard from you in over two months, and I will keep my promise to myself and not mail you again. I am talking to myself through you now. I hope that you are happy. I suspect that you are not. I had a fantasy that perhaps you had come to find me, to bring me home. But I know this fantasy for what it is. And I know that only I can lead myself home.

Home – what a big word that is. Perhaps the biggest of words. I think of our home sometimes, the big house in Auteuil with the stained-glass front-door that turned the sunlight on our hands and arms red and green and blue; the overstuffed faded-yellow sofa in the day room where we would huddle together by the fire, whilst nanny read us Blanche Neige, La Belle au Bois

Dormant and Cendrillon. I remember the red-velvet drapes in Papa's study where I would hide, hopping from foot to foot, shivering with excitement and the cold, knowing that you would find me there, but still screaming with mock outrage when you did. I recall the secret cupboard by the attic stairs that we made our own, the green-satin throw that we crept beneath in the semi-darkness to survey our latest treasures, the sou that we found at Uncle Emile's farm that we knew had been hidden there by a soldier so that he had money to reach his long-lost love after the war, the ancient, dusty, black book that smelled of dried leaves that we stole from Madame Chavanelle's classroom because it was written in a language that we knew held the secrets to all that was mysterious and unsolved in life. I remember the big oval mirror with the gilt frame, chipped at the bottom, in Mama's old room, where we were not allowed to go but into which we would steal to gaze at ourselves side by side, each trying to outstare the other, losing ourselves in one another's identical blue eyes, knowing and feeling what it meant to be twins. Perelle, I have no yearning for the house itself because I have a visceral and physical sense of the spaces and the secrets and the mysteries that we shared there as children, as though they live on within my very body, as though I am that house and you live inside of me. I hear echoes of your laughter, your voice, the sound of your feet running on the stairs, the sound of your breathing as you sleep, and it is only for the sense of you that I yearn, Perelle, because you are my home.

I feel very old and very young. Sometimes I am able to sit still, watch and listen, to observe a calmness and a stillness that I never before noticed. Before, I saw only the vibration and hum of everything, the quivering, pulsating beat of life. The stillness I now perceive may be inside of me or outside; it is difficult to tell because it is so quiet here. And I realise how tired I was. How tired of running; running away, running towards, being in perpetual motion that didn't take me anywhere. There is an ebb and a flow to everything. The yogi told me this, and I felt the truth of his words instantly. My river has flowed into this lake and here I must swim a while whilst I try to understand this word 'home'.

Chapter 33 – Gina

It wakes her in the night. Once again the memory has assaulted her in her sleep. She is sweating and shaking. She tries to smoke but can't still her shaking hand. Please no, she thinks. Please no. She wants the dream to go, but more than that she wants this thing not to be true. It is dark. Rachel isn't here. Richard isn't here.

The morning arrived like a train crash, and Gina both welcomed and cursed it, waking with that hollow, sickly feeling that follows a disturbed night. She had no idea what time it was and couldn't be bothered to look. She groped for her cigarettes, found them and her lighter amid the chaos on her bedside table. I should quit, she thought as she lit a cigarette, closed her eyes and inhaled deeply.

She was in no hurry to get up. Instead she lay back on her pillows and stared up at the ceiling, watching the smoke she was exhaling curling away from her in meandering coils. She tried to think about the days behind her and the days ahead. She considered the events of yesterday. She was appalled with herself. She closed her eyes and tried to remember when Rachel was coming back.

Several cigarettes later Gina heaved herself off the bed and padded through to the kitchen. She was wearing a nightshirt but she didn't remember getting changed into it. The French doors were closed, and shafts of dappled light glanced through the shutters giving the kitchen a shady and somehow Italian feel. She lit a cigarette and began to smoke it as she made coffee, listlessly collecting the cup, the bottled water, heaping too much coffee onto the spoon but not caring. Yawning, Gina walked through to the anteroom with the cup and opened the French doors. And here was the relentless, inevitable heat, almost at its fiercest since it looked to be about noon. The hot tiles savaged her bare feet, but she couldn't be bothered to go inside and get flip-flops. An ashtray was already on the floor, and Gina flopped onto a chair. The chair cushion felt hot against her thighs through the fabric of her nightshirt. She sipped her coffee and took a long drag of her cigarette.

Yesterday had forced Gina to acknowledge that she wasn't coping. It frightened her. She was usually so in control, so capable, that she wasn't sure how to react to herself. It was strangely ironic, she thought grimly, that some part of herself had allowed her to fall apart when there was no one here who could take care of her, when she was alone and at her most vulnerable. Gina looked over the balcony. A brown man was sweeping the red path with a stick brush, his back bent to the job. She took a deep breath. What she needed, Gina decided, trying to draw up reserves of characteristic focus, was a plan.

But a plan seemed far too grand a thing. She decided instead simply to stay here for a while on the balcony. The searing sun injured her skin. She remembered that she had left her sun cream by the pool when wanting to get away from Dave. She didn't care. She watched a large, colourful bird swoop out of one tree and into another. The branches shook and then stopped. She watched the man with the brush finish his sweeping, glance at his watch and hurry off towards the reception area. His shirt was very white, his skin very dark. She watched a big green lizard sitting perfectly still on the balcony wall opposite hers. She looked away and when she looked back it had gone. She watched some German guests walking along the path talking quietly, carrying big blue beach-towels. One had yellow flowers on it. The husband was very tall, the wife very small. She nodded a lot. He frowned. She watched a black fly walk all the way along the balcony rail, its impossibly delicate legs scurrying along, stopping every so often to rub its antennae together.

Gina watched herself watching. She was aware of the sun moving towards the sea. She sighed and ground her spent cigarette savagely into the ashtray, got up, and went inside, leaving it and the mug on the balcony. She looked around her. The place was tidy; the room boys had been in yesterday while she was out. Gina went through to the bedroom and switched on the fan. It made a rasping, grating sound as it whirred haltingly into action. She didn't like the light in the bedroom; it was dirty and jarring. She needed to dress and go somewhere. So she walked into the bathroom and showered quickly, washed her hair, brushing it back from her face when she stepped out from under the warm water. She tried to tie her hair in a knot the way she had seen Indian women wear their hair. But hers wasn't long enough, so she used one of Rachel's scrunchies and tied it into a tight ponytail instead.

In the bedroom she rummaged amongst her clothes whilst wearing a towel and eventually found a bikini, rummaged around again and found a sarong and a tee-shirt – one of the ones she had bought from a roadside stall about a week ago. She had liked the colours, muted oranges and yellows, cheerful but not brash, she had thought. Now the tee-shirt made her sick. But she pulled it over her head and stepped into her flip-flops. She grabbed her red-mirrored bag and stuffed in her cigarettes, lighter and her door-key which she found on her bedside table. Her purse and phone were already in the bag. She noted herself checking all these things and laughed out loud, a short, hostile bark. She hated herself for all this checking, but didn't know why. She left their rooms, closing the door firmly behind her.

Once down the stairs, Gina turned left and walked along the red path towards the swimming pool, her sandals making a satisfying plopping sound with each step. She and Rachel hadn't spent much time together here, only the first afternoon whilst they got their bearings and adjusted to the temperature and the time difference. At the pool a few middle-aged and elderly couples were lying prone on sunloungers. The German pair was nowhere to be seen. Gina looked around and was pleased that Dave didn't appear to be here. A fat, bald man was lazily breaststroking his way across the pool. Gina thought about going back for her beach towel, but a serving boy hurried over with a towel for her and held out his arm to indicate that she should take her choice of loungers. Gina nodded at him and took the towel. She made her way to a lounger in the far corner away from the other guests. The serving boy followed and asked Gina quietly if he could get her a drink, any snacks. She ordered a gin and tonic. It arrived five minutes later in a clear plastic glass. Gina was pleased that the drink was cold. The boy disappeared discreetly without lingering for a tip.

Having drunk half of her drink, Gina worried briefly about not having any sun cream. She wondered how long she could sit here in the heat without having to cool down in the pool. There was a loud splashing sound as the bald man heaved himself out at the far end. Gina thought he looked like a walrus and wondered vaguely what nationality he was. Swedish she thought, or perhaps German. Definitely not British. She lay back on the lounger. She had spread the towel out on top of it and taken off her sarong. She felt hot and uncomfortable.

Her thoughts turned to the last time she had been on holiday with Richard. It had been early autumn last year, and they had taken a last-minute trip to Greece, to the tiny island of Poros. They only had a week and had hired mopeds to take them around the hilly little island. It was beautiful in a timeless, lazy way, and they had a mellow time, discovering ruined temples, laughing at the goats among the rocks with their tinkling neck-bells and quizzical looks. They stole oranges from trees, made up stories about the people they saw and drank wine on secluded beaches. These gentle, intimate adventures intensified their relationship, and Gina had felt close to Richard and very much in love. They had spent a night on a small, quiet beach. They had brought the itchy green guest-room blankets with them and had eaten cheese and olives, drunk red wine and made love right there on the beach under the stars, the ancient Aegean hissing rhythmic encouragement beside them. They had decided that night that one day they would marry. Gina sighed. She closed her eyes and thought of the last night she had spent on a beach.

A crashing splash interrupted Gina's reverie and she sat upright with a start as she was splattered with water from the pool. She frowned in annoyance as she watched the walrus's great back bob its unwieldy hulk from her side of the pool towards the far end. She wondered irritably why it was that men so often found it necessary to make such effusive aquatic entrances. The sun was blazing down, and Gina was anxious about becoming even more burnt. She thought about going in for a swim, but seeing the walrus bobbing back towards her, decided against it. Instead she beckoned the waiter over and ordered another gin and tonic. It arrived almost immediately and Gina drank it with small, quick sips. The familiar warmth of her second drink made her arms feel heavy. It was not an unpleasant feeling, and Gina closed her eyes.

She became aware of spicy aromas coming from the direction of the dining area and tried to decide whether she was hungry. But she couldn't bring herself to feel enthusiastic about eating and instead drained the last of her drink and stood up. She wrapped her sarong around her waist and slipped her feet into her sandals.

The beach was at the end of a long, narrow pathway that led from the back of the hotel complex, past the gardens of another, smaller hotel and eventually past some scrubland and down to the sand. Between the two hotels were a few wood-and-thatch shacks selling hand-sewn Indian clothing and various pretty trinkets. Next to these was a larger shack where massages and other beauty treatments were available. Gina left the confines of the pool and the hotel and wandered up the pathway. The barman was polishing a glass as she passed, and he raised his hand to her, nodding politely. Gina nodded back. She walked past the first couple of shacks, shaking her head when the young girls outside them started to approach her. But she paused at the massage shack, where a man in a short-sleeved white shirt and a lungi was reading a newspaper at a small desk. in front of him were burning incense and small statues of Ganesh and Shiva. The man put his newspaper down when he saw Gina and hurried over.

'You like massage?' he asked. 'Good massage, plenty cheap for you.'

Gina slowed down and looked at the man, squinting her eyes in the sun.

There were massage shacks all over the district, and Gina and Rachel had talked about visiting one. Gina hovered now, looking at the man and at the shack.

'Come, please come.'

The man was quietly insistent. Gina was led to the desk, where she was invited to sit down on a wooden chair whilst the man told her about all the different massage variations that were on offer and what they would cost. He spoke in a hushed, almost reverent voice and didn't hurry her. The smell of incense was sweet and intoxicating, and Gina felt as though she were somehow falling into it. He explained to her that the masseurs were trained in all aspects of Ayurvedic massage. The man suggested to Gina that a full-body massage would be good for her body and her soul. She was shown to another wooden seat where the man asked her to wait whilst he fetched the masseur. She thought with resignation that she really didn't care whether she had this massage or not, so she may as well go along with it and allow the man to make his sale. He returned seconds later with a slight, demure-looking young woman of about twenty who was wearing a pale-coloured salwaar kameez. The man indicated that Gina should follow her. Gina did as she was asked and followed the woman into a little room made of thatch. The wooden door was closed behind them.

Inside was a long wooden table covered with a clean strip of material. The girl evidently spoke very little English but indicated with a delicate flourish of her hand that Gina should undress. The girl didn't turn away, and trying to appear worldlier than she felt, Gina removed her sarong and her tee-shirt and placed them carefully onto a chair with her bag. The girl indicated that Gina should remove her bikini as well. Trying to conceal her embarrassment, Gina complied. The young woman approached her, took her gently by the shoulders in a curiously intimate manner and turned her around. She took the scrunchy gently from Gina's hair and smoothed it out slowly with her fingers. Gina shivered. The girl laid it on top of Gina's things and then motioned to her to climb onto the table and lie down on her back.

Once prone on the table, Gina took a deep breath and closed her eyes. She shifted her shoulders and her hips in an attempt to get comfortable on the hard surface. The young woman was clearly at ease as she set about massaging Gina's limbs, hot from the sun, in long, slow strokes with the practicality and simplicity of someone very practiced. Gina began to relax. The oil the young woman smoothed into her skin smelt of coconut and jasmine, beautiful, sensual, melding scents which flowed into the heady scent of the incense burning outside. Gina could hear the occasional rattling cry of the wiry little Macaque monkeys, the constant twittering and whistling of many birds. The young woman stroked the fragrant oil into Gina's stomach. Her hands felt hot on her abdomen and she seemed to linger there. Gina opened her eyes. Above her she could see the light glancing obliquely through the gaps in the woven-thatch roof of the shack, casting a mix of shade and verdant light over her naked body. She felt very warm, enveloped in this earthy, corporeal, essentially female experience.

This was not the passive peace and quiet that accompanied massages at home, Gina thought, as she relaxed further. This was very different from those carried out by clinically attired, judicious women in expensive pastel settings to a background of generic relaxation music. This was an elemental, sensual, experience, robust in its physicality. Gina felt stripped, pared down to her basic, fundamental being. She closed her eyes again and wondered where the tears were, and realised with a sense of numb abstraction that she was both full and completely empty.

Chapter 34 – Rachel

The train clattered on and on and gave Rachel time to think. She wasn't sure that she wanted this, but Pravi had fallen asleep and there was nothing to distract her from her thoughts. She stared out of the window and into the red earth. It made her think of blood. As they left Mumbai behind them, the city seemed to her to be an aberration, something heavy and perverted in the midst of this naïve and ancient harmony. It had dislodged something in her, and its dark, sludgy survival had seeped into her insidiously. The complex snare of emotions and perceptions she had undergone there made her feel both more and less whole than before.

As the train rocked on, Rachel was aware of feeling edgy and apprehensive. She thought seriously about Gina now that there was no putting it off. The train was hurtling inexorably towards the time when she would have to deal with her, with whatever had or hadn't happened to her on the beach, at the very least her anger at having been left behind in Kanyakumari. She wondered whether their friendship could be repaired, but wasn't even sure that it was broken. Rachel's uncertainty about Gina threw a new and unwelcome dimension into their relationship. It was barbed with anger as well as apprehension, and it made her feel guilty again. She frowned, not wanting to have to confront such conflict. But she knew she had to resign herself to talking with Gina, explaining, justifying, trying to understand. She hoped that they wouldn't argue. She realised that she had been clenching her fists and held her palms open in front of her, looked down at the little red-crescent indentations left by her nails. She stared heavily out of the window and sighed once more.

Rachel looked across at Pravi dozing in his seat. She thought about the time they had spent together, the wild things they had done and not done, the uncertainties she had felt and recovered from. She couldn't quite fathom this young man. Despite his excellent English, their communication was often rudimentary, clunky. But at other times it was piercing, punishing in its acuity. With him she had laughed more than with anyone on this trip, but still, she felt his presence to be weighty, profound and as such, tiring. She looked at Pravi's face, gentle in sleep, the tender bulge of his eyes beneath their lids vulnerable and defenceless and felt that she wanted to escape from him.

A group of backpackers swayed along the carriage consulting their tickets and talking loudly in Australian accents before coming to a stop by the seats opposite Rachel. They smiled a lot, their eyes and mouths wide, and made a big commotion of heaving their backpacks into the bunks above before flopping into the seats, their long legs carelessly flung in front of them. Rachel smiled at the men, glad of the interruption. They were three men all in their mid to late twenties she supposed. 'G'day,' one of them said to her.

'Hi,' said Rachel, trying to keep some of the enthusiasm out of her voice.

'Hot outside.' His platitude seemed to her a marvel of innocence. She nodded and smiled encouragingly.

'We were sat in the wrong seats,' one of the men explained. 'Got moved on. Think these are ours though.'

The men got themselves comfortable and chatted amongst themselves for a while. Rachel looked at Pravi who was still asleep. She took the band off her hair and shook it out.

After a while one of the Australians turned again to Rachel.

'Where a ya headed?' he asked, his voice a soporific drawl. Rachel smiled broadly and raised her eyebrows as Pravi had done to her.

'Kanyakumari,' she replied. 'And you?'

'Bonzer, yeah us too. Helluvva trip,' said the blonder of the three men, 'and then on up into the hills for a bit in Tamil Nadu.'

Rachel was intrigued.

'Well I doh know 'bout you lot,' the darkest one of the three said, 'but I'm about ready for a beer!'

Beer was produced, opened, handed around, and Rachel accepted a bottle. It had a picture of a snake on the label.

'Man, I was parched! I'm Marcus,' said one of the dark-haired men, holding out a big hand. Rachel took it. 'This here is Ben.'

Ben saluted her.

'And this is Paul.'

'Good to meet ya,' Paul said.

'And what might your name be?' asked Marcus.

'I'm Rachel,' she replied.

'Well, Rachel,' said Marcus. 'Glad to make your acquaintance. Sure beats looking at these two ugly mugs the whole journey!'

The men were postgraduate students at the University of Queensland. All were training to be mechanical engineers and were on holiday from university, having just taken exams.

'We just got here last week,' Paul told her. 'Been in Mumbai. Man, whadda place! Spent most of our time in

Leopolds. Good bar, that. Great beer.' He nodded to no one in particular.

Ben told her that they were planning to spend a month travelling in India before he and Paul went back to Australia and Marcus flew to the UK to meet up with some cousins who were working in London. 'We're planning on travelling in the south for a bit.'

Rachel shifted in her set so that she was facing them. 'Where will you go after Kanyakumari?' she asked.

'No fixed plan,' answered Ben. 'Prob'ly head back north, get to Pondicherry eventually, then across to Bangalore and then to Goa. Spend the last week chilling there on the beach with plenty of these.'

He raised his bottle of beer, and the others did the same. Rachel smiled and took a swig of hers.

'You here on your own, then?' asked Marcus, running a hand across his cropped hair and swigging back the last of his beer.

'You got another one of those, Ben? Grab one for Rache.'

Rachel liked the way he shortened her name.

'I came here with my friend Gina,' Rachel answered. 'She's back in Kanyakumari. She didn't want to come to Mumbai with us.'

'Gina, eh? No worries,' said Marcus. 'You're not joined at the hip.' Ben handed her another bottle of beer which he had opened for her.

Pravi continued to loll in his seat, his lips slightly open, a bead of saliva hovering in the corner of his mouth, his eyelids flickering weakly, harmless in sleep. These men appeared to Rachel as bright and as welcome as sunrise after a long, dark night. Their talk was all flash and banter, and it relieved her to be a part of it.

'That yer boyfriend?' Marcus asked gesturing with his beer bottle towards Pravi.

'Man, this beer's going down a treat. Break out some more will ya, Paul mate.'

Rachel was handed another bottle, and she took a large gulp. The assumption that Pravi was her boyfriend bothered her, and she wasn't sure why. Or maybe she was.

'No,' she replied, 'he's just a friend. We met a week or so ago and decided to do some travelling together.'

'That's cool,' Marcus said, nodding. 'Gives the trip a kick when you hook up with diff'rent people like that.'

The others agreed.

At Ratnagiri, Ben decided that they needed more beer, and he and Paul dashed out onto the busy station to buy some from a small, skinny man with a cool-box strapped to a bicycle. Pravi was still asleep.

'So, Rache,' Marcus said. 'Just you and me.'

Rachel smiled broadly, enjoying the way the beer was making her feel.

'You know, we should hook up in Kanyakumari. Hit the bars. Be a buzz.'

'Great,' she answered.

'Bring yer friend too. What's her name? Gina? Paint the town. Place won't know what's hit it. Bring yer boyfriend if ya like.'

He nodded towards Pravi, who stirred in sleep, turning his face towards the window. Rachel rolled her eyes and pretended to slap Marcus with the back of her hand.

'Man, it's a freakin oven out there!'

Ben and Paul struggled back along the carriage and into their seats, both carrying four bottles of beer in each hand.

'These should keep us going for a while,' Ben said, handing a bottle to Rachel.

As the train rocked on, Rachel and the men chatted. They told her about university life in Queensland. They compared places they had been, and Rachel listened to stories about places she hadn't been. The students seemed to have spent a lot of time camping in the outback – 'the great Australian interior' as Ben called it. They told stories about their encounters with the 'abos', some of which made Rachel feel uncomfortable. She decided to overlook this. The men seemed to have a relaxed attitude towards the places they visited and travelled through. They didn't seem to expect to give or to receive much from the different cultures and people they encountered, but rather they appeared to travel inside a bubble, retaining their own outlook and beliefs about the world and their place in it, which were sustained by the presence of one another. She took a long swig of her beer and smiled. These men seemed so carefree – they didn't seem to be seeking anything – merely looking. It felt refreshing to her after the intensity and variety of emotion she had experienced with Pravi.

'Where a you headed after Kanyakumari?' Paul asked.

And then, like daybreak, there it was, cast in sharp relief before her. Simple! The thought crystallised from out of the red earth and the sleeping man before her, from out of the backpacks in the overhead bunk, from the laughter of these carefree young men. It snaked out of the bottle in her hand and laughed at her, beckoned her and tempted her with its nakedness, its simplicity, its precision and candour. She wouldn't go home with

Gina, she would stay here in India and go travelling with these men!

Chapter 35 – Gina

She was on the beach again, but she wasn't sure how long she'd been there. She looked at the sunloungers, innocent in their daytime occupations, affording comfort and rest to the contented visitors. Brown men were walking up and down hessian pathways, carrying drinks and snacks to the sunbathers. Friendly banter was exchanged, smiles. Gina didn't make eye contact with anyone. How different it all looked in the daytime. The one thing that remained the same was the vast, swollen sea behind it all, which continued to make a mockery of the little concerns of the lives of the people on its insignificant shore.

She sat at the shack, staring and smoking, the remains of a glass of gin in one hand. Her throat ached, and Gina didn't know if it was thirst or the effect of so much recent effort not to cry. But she couldn't summon the motivation to order water. She wanted nothing more at this moment than to be in Richard's arms, for him to take care of her, to take it all away. She looked at the beach. It threw back at her the word that Gina needed to articulate, the word that would begin her journey towards acceptance of the thing they had done. She could contain it no longer. Everything in her had conspired against the thought of the word that threatened to undo her, to destroy her with its savage import.

Time passed. Gina smoked, staring straight ahead at the beckoning sea. When her cigarette was spent she ground it out and stood. She put her sparkly red bag carefully on the chair then walked slowly towards the water's edge. She stood there gazing out to sea before dropping her gaze to the sand where she saw a little shell and for some reason stooped to pick it up.

Chapter 36 – Rachel

My god, she thought, staring at the empty beer bottle in front of her. Why not? Surely the practicalities could be worked out, changing her return ticket, talking to her boss, to Gina. Really, why not?

'Are you serious?' Ben had asked, and when she'd replied that, yes, she was very serious, they had all laughed and said things like 'Bonzer' and 'Jeeze, man!' in a way that had made her feel exciting and daring. She hadn't told them much about her situation, choosing instead to gloss over the fact that she and Gina were due to fly home in a few days' time. Instead she presented the idea of travelling with them as something that fitted in well with her own plans.

'I'd love to go with you. Since Gina is going back soon, it will be great to have some new travelling companions for a while,' she said.

As the words left her mouth, she thought that they were surely the most exciting words she had ever uttered. The four of them chattered happily about where they would go, what they would do and see. She threw herself into the banter and hardly recognised herself. As she talked on about what she would see in her trip around India, she barely noticed India passing by outside the window.

The Australians exchanged mobile numbers and email addresses with Rachel and, having established that their hostel was in the centre of Kanyakumari, arranged to meet up the following evening at a bar. Rachel had in mind one that she and Gina had been to with Pravi and his friends about a week ago. She felt pleased with herself for being able to suggest a place to meet. She felt every bit the experienced traveller in India.

Pravi woke up, yawning luxuriantly, and stretched his arms over his head. He smiled at Rachel in a sleepy way.

'Hi,' she said to him, feeling awkward as she saw the Australians eyeing him curiously.

'Pravi, these are Marcus, Ben and Paul,' she gabbled. 'They're from Australia.'

Rachel felt uncomfortable as she introduced him to her new friends perhaps somewhat too quickly. For some reason she felt defensive about them. Pravi was polite and courteous but reserved as he sat up in his seat and greeted the Australians. He seemed to lack the interest he had shown in Vish. Rachel felt more than a little apprehensive about telling Pravi of her new travel plan, and she wondered why. She thought that she may as well get it over with, and she spoke to him in bright, brittle tones, telling him how exciting this change of plan would be for her. The Australians grinned. 'Whad'dya think, mate?' Ben asked him.

It sounded like a challenge. Pravi glanced at the empty beer bottles on the table and levelled an intense stare at Rachel. He said nothing.

It felt like a long time since Rachel and Gina had met Pravi. they'd been at a bar and Pravi was sitting at a table on his own. She had asked him to join them. He'd smiled graciously and done so, and Rachel had watched him as he stood, noting with furtive pleasure the dark skin of his neck, the top of his chest against the white of his kurta. Pravi was waiting for some friends, and when they arrived they had ordered drinks and had laughed and joked together before one of the group suggested that they all go on to another nearby bar. Rachel and Gina had gone with them, and the evening had been spent enjoying the novelty and spark of this new and stimulating company. Before going back to their hotel, Rachel and Pravi had swapped mobile numbers with the intention of making plans for them all to meet up the next day.

Since that initial meeting, Rachel, Gina, Pravi and Pravi's friends had spent a lot of time together, and now of course Rachel had spent the past four days with him. But, she reasoned to herself, she owed nothing to this man. They were two free individuals who had met by chance and who had chosen to spend some time together. They had enjoyed the time that they had, and now she was moving on. Although Rachel could see nothing wrong in that, the words that Pravi had spoken in the café in Mumbai came back and taunted her. 'You don't connect with people deeply for long. You leave them behind.'

Chapter 37 – Sandrine

This morning we were woken at five by the bell and I got up straight away. By seven we had hiked to the sea where we sat meditating and chanting for around forty minutes. It was a wonderful way to begin the day. We did pranayama and yoga when we got back for around an hour and a half, and then we ate some bananas.

I am enjoying the feeling of aloneness. I am maintaining my silence as the yogi told me, and I know that it is taking me farther and farther away from Perelle. That is good. I begin to see my silence in the trees, in the stones, in the butterflies that land here and there and that never stop for long. I hear my silence in the beating of the Tablas and in the morning wake-up bell. It is in the chanting, in the incense, in the spices that flavour our food and in the cool water that we drink.

A lecture is about to begin. We are sitting on the thatched rooftop, with views to the right of lushly forested mountains. I can see the yellow roofs of a temple on the top of the highest peak. I am thinking of the idea of bringing inner knowledge in line with experience. The word 'yoga' means 'union'. The lecturer is talking about the concept of God, and it is raining hard. It makes the distant hills misty. Heavy drops of rain are dripping off the thatched roof. I suddenly see that power is rushing into the human body. Into all material things in fact.

The yogi is here now. 'Absolute truth is formless,' he said. 'The mind uses forms in order to better understand. The spirit is not us; we are the spirit.' He told me that a mantra is a sound that can protect us. It helps to tune our mind and our thoughts to the universal. He told me that no one ever refuses positive energy. 'If someone offered you something positive,' he asked, 'would you ever say no?' I remember his smile as he said that. 'People who are free to choose always choose peace.'

I am enjoying being silent and still, as the yogi said I would. He was right. I find that I am able to direct my mind towards those things that need my attention and away from those which do not. He trained me well. It is a good thing to be able to keep one's own silence amid the noise of others. When I listen to some of the conversations, I notice that they are often descriptions of states of mind and opinions. I think these conversations may be barriers. They are often negative in content. They mask one's silence. Better, I think, to reflect inwardly.

The lecture is about Vedic mathematics. I have learned that there are other methods to reach the correct answers to mathematical problems. It reminds me that there are many routes to enlightenment. I feel my silence descending, enveloping me. It feels like a refuge, a relief. I have realised that I have nothing to say, or that it doesn't matter if I say nothing. In silence we are able to listen, to hear, to absorb and to learn. To grow. My silence is becoming full and complete. It is thickening around me, viscous and malleable.

The yogi told me about Saraswati: that she is Brahma's wife and the goddess of wisdom and science. He asked me to think about her. She has four arms. In one hand she presents a flower to her husband. In another she holds a book of palm leaves, indicating learning. In a left hand she has a string of pearls – a japa. And in the other a small drum. Sometimes she is depicted playing a stringed instrument and is seated on a lotus flower. She dwells on earth amongst men, but her home is with her husband in Brahmaloka. Her name means 'watery' and she is a river deity. 'Her opulent waters command tides,' he said. 'She is mistress of wealth and progeny. She possesses power and immortality.' He asked Saraswati to bestow her vitality on us, her worshipers.

A butterfly is fluttering above our heads as the Vedic-mathematics professor explains his methods. They both have something to teach us. They both have messages.

'Truth in itself is simple,' he says. 'We find it by cutting out the complications.'

Chapter 38 – Rachel

The train rattled through the night, and Rachel and the others dozed in their bunks, negotiating their own personal cramps and cricks through their fractured dreams. Rachel's dreams lurched along a bumpy track, and she couldn't keep up with them. She kept trying to grasp something, to comprehend something, but couldn't quite name it, and when she thought she could see it, understand the picture, the words, the colour of their essence drained away and with it its meaning. She was left with nothing but an unsatisfactory feeling, something approaching impatience. It exhausted her, and in her almost-awake state she felt testy and drained.

Morning had stolen into the carriage and nudged her awake, and looking around Rachel had seen that Pravi and the Australians were all still asleep. She thought of a nest of kittens, and this made her smile. Outside, the day looked washed and translucent. Rachel rummaged in her backpack for her toilet bag, trying not to make too much noise, extricated herself carefully from her bunk and made her way along the carriage. She felt glad to be alone as she swayed past the sleeping passengers. She freshened up as best she could in the grim little toilet and then stood for a while in the carriage intersection, stretching and looking out at the passing landscape. She wondered which state they were in, whether they had passed yet from Maharastra into Goa. She wondered what the rest of south India would be like. Would it be red? Was all of India red? One of the Australians – Paul, she thought – had described Kerala as 'temple central', and Rachel had thought greedily of all that she would see there. She thought fleetingly now with some brief regret that Pravi wouldn't be there to help her to try to see it from the inside. But it might be nice, she thought, to see the place without trying to understand it all. When you don't fully comprehend something, she thought, you are less responsible, freer.

Rachel accepted coffee from a vendor who was passing through the carriages and sipped it slowly as she stood and watched the world waking up. When she finished, she waited until the same vendor came back and asked for another cup. In the last few days she hadn't slept much or deeply, and she felt as though she were running on caffeine and adrenalin, tetchy and brittle. She continued to gaze out of the window and marvelled briefly at intermittent groups of women carrying rush baskets full of rubble and stones on their heads. Construction workers. Road workers. But without machinery to aid them. She watched men pounding long sticks into the ground to dig holes. There seemed to be hoards of them toiling listlessly in the morning heat. Rachel supposed that eventually the sun would get too hot to work in and they would have to stop. Or maybe not, she thought.

When she eventually made her way back to her seat, she found Marcus awake.

'Hey babe,' he said and winked at her, all vowels and squashy brashness.

She smiled. 'It's a beautiful morning,' she said.

'S'pose iddiz,' Marcus answered, flicking a glance out of the window. 'Ya manage ta sleep much?'

'No, not really,' Rachel answered. 'Did you?'

'Nah. Bloody uncomfortable foreign trains!' His voice rolled around the carriage. 'Indians are bloody tiny. Tiny bunks are no good for a strapping lad like me! No one my size could get a decent kip on one a these!'

He slapped the bunk and stretched. Rachel looked at Pravi who was still sleeping soundly on his bunk and thought, but didn't say, that he was about the same size as Marcus.

Their voices roused the other Australians, and they stretched and yawned and greeted one another and Rachel loudly before shambling off to the toilet. Rachel heard 'Man, whadda nite' and 'Jeez, Ben, you look like shit!' as they lurched towards the end of the carriage.

Pravi opened his eyes. He smiled at Rachel, a slow, sleepy, sexy smile, she thought, before she could check herself. She smiled back and wondered how long he had been awake. Neither of them said anything.

After a while the Australians returned. 'Jeez man, it's hot.'

Some of the sparkle seemed to Rachel to have left this observation since Marcus last commented on the temperature. She tried to think of her new adventure.

'So, Rache,' the abbreviation scratched her, 'you know Kanyakumari. Be there soon. You still up for this drink then?'

Rachel and the Australians had agreed the night before, while Pravi was dozing, to go together from the station to Kanyakumari and have a few drinks before the Australians went to find their hostel.

'We can go to Dreams if you like,' Rachel said now. 'It has a relaxed vibe.' She heard herself using the word 'vibe' and smiled inwardly. 'It's near the main beachfront. We can get something to eat near there as well if you like?'

'Dreams eh? Good name. We have to go there!' Paul hooted, winking at the others.

'Sure thing, babe, sounds good ta me,' Marcus said.

'You up f'rit, Ben?'

Ben was.

'Rachel, come with me, please.'

Pravi was quiet but firm. Marcus put on a shocked face. Rachel raised her eyebrows at him and rolled her eyes, although she felt bad doing it. She stood and followed Pravi, swaying along the carriages until they reached the intersection.

'Rachel, I would like to talk before we go our separate ways. Will you have chai with me when we arrive in Kanyakumari?'

His precise annunciation annoyed her. 'Pravi, I've arranged to go for a drink with the guys. You and I have talked for days; we've had a great time, we really have. But I'm going with them now.'

'Rachel, we have enjoyed our time together, that's true, but I would like to talk. Please.' He sounded like a schoolteacher. 'We can't talk here. You can meet your new friends afterwards. I am only asking for half an hour more from you. That is all.'

Chapter 39 – Sandrine

I am looking for signs and messages now. I have a feel for my direction. There is a sense in which I need no signs, since the truth and the way are clear and apparent, but signs can be affirming. I am looking for more words although I know that they will come in their own time. When I have them I will use them. For now my silence continues.

All around are signs and sights of activity. We are like a hive, all working together for the greater good of the ashram. I am sitting outside the lower hall. It is cool here. I am debating whether or not to eat this evening. I think perhaps not. The yogi told me that every cell in our bodies is working as hard as it can to keep us functioning and healthy and alive. Our cells love us! We are their god and we must respect this and treat our bodies with gratitude. And so I will now be careful what I put into my body and for a while I will have only one meal each day.

It is so very green here. The fronds of the palms and the leaves of the trees and the plants are waving gently in the warm breeze. I am sitting in the shade of a banana tree drinking spiced tea. After the yoga session, a woman spoke to me about how difficult she is finding the asana. I had watched her trying a headstand, and her limbs were loose and uncontrolled. I resisted the urge to tell her this, and instead I simply smiled. I find that my silence becomes a companion. I am able to enter into an internal dialogue, which moves me forward. Dialogue with others rarely does this, since generally we require affirmations or victories. An inner dialogue requires no such outcomes. The yogi said yesterday that there are many languages but only one silence. I understand that silence unifies us. In silence we are one.

Chapter 40 – Rachel

The train lurched and screeched to a protesting halt at the station in Kanyakumari. All the remaining passengers were disembarking, and Rachel, Pravi and the three Australians stood up and collected their belongings, stuffing them into their backpacks, before heaving them onto their shoulders and joining the throng snaking its way slowly off the train.

'Six o'clock, Rache, Dreams,' Marcus said when they were on the crowded platform. 'Don't be late!' He raised his hand in a high five, and Rachel reciprocated rather self-consciously. He held onto her raised hand for a fraction longer than was necessary, held her eyes with his. Pravi watched, his expression not betraying his thoughts.

'Come on dude, there's a taxi here!' Ben was gesturing at the others whilst trying to wedge his backpack into the back seat of a waiting maruti van.

'See'ya man,' Marcus said to Pravi.

'Six o'clock, Rache!' he called as he hurried over to the other two.

'I'll be there!' Rachel called back.

Once out of the station, they walked for some way before Pravi found a café and led Rachel inside and up some stairs. It was air-conditioned and Rachel was grateful for the cool blast of air against her sticky skin. Plastic tables and red padded bench-seats were set out in booths in an L-shape. They took seats at the far end around the corner. Only one other table was occupied by a group of young men who looked up briefly as

Rachel and Pravi passed. Pravi ordered chai for them both.

Moments passed and Pravi didn't seem in any hurry to talk. Eventually Rachel felt that she couldn't wait anymore. She was impatient to leave, to get back to the Australians.

'Okay Pravi, what is it you want to say?'

Pravi didn't answer straight away but sipped his drink slowly, blowing across its milky surface once or twice to cool it down. Rachel felt he was playing with her. She held her breath and exhaled slowly. She drank her own chai. She slipped off her sandals under the table and rubbed her feet together.

'Rachel,' Pravi said at last, 'what are you doing?'

Rachel thought for a fraction of a second that he was referring to her having taken off her sandals, but she quickly grasped his meaning. She put her elbow on the table in front of her, looked down and frowned, put her head on one side and brushed her hair from her face. Then she folded her arms and leant back, a gesture of defiance.

'What do you mean?' she said, trying to sound nonchalant, but failing. 'I'm not doing anything.'

'You understand me, Rachel. Why are you doing this? What about Gina?'

The name was a slap.

'What do you mean "What about Gina?"' she answered. 'What about her?'

'Rachel, Gina is your friend. Will you abandon her still further?'

Her fury caught her unawares and she flung her answer back at him. 'Abandon her further? That's rich coming from you. You were perfectly happy for me to go to Mumbai with you! How is it okay for me to go with you, but it isn't okay for me to go travelling with anyone else?'

Pravi didn't speak for a while. He seemed to be considering his words, and when he did speak his voice was quieter still. 'Rachel, please think about what it is you are proposing to do. You don't know these men. You are taking a risk. And your friend needs you.'

'And I wasn't taking a risk going away with you?' She spat the words at him. 'Why is this any different? And what do you know about what Gina needs? She's my friend not yours; you don't know her. You don't know me. You certainly don't have the right to patronise me or to tell me how to conduct myself. I am capable enough to make my own decisions!'

Rachel was trying to keep her voice low. She didn't want a scene here in the café, but her rage was gathering momentum. Pravi remained calm and this incensed her further. She felt herself grinding her teeth. Her arms were still folded and she was clenching one of her thumbs in her tightly balled fist.

Pravi looked sad. 'I am speaking as a friend, Rachel, not as an enemy. You don't have to take my advice, that is true. And you are right, of course; there is a lot I don't know about you and about Gina. But Rachel,' he paused, looked at her intently, 'you were frightened of me in that apartment in Mumbai. I could feel your fear. I could hear it in your voice, and I could see it in your eyes. And Rachel, you were right to be frightened. Not because I would have harmed you. But because I could have harmed you. You were vulnerable; you were completely defenceless, Rachel. It wasn't your good judgement that kept you safe there in that flat in Mumbai where no one knew your whereabouts. It was mine.'

He let the words do their work. Rachel was shocked.

'What are you saying?' she said quietly, deflated now. 'That you wanted to hurt me?'

'No Rachel, I am not saying that I wanted to hurt you. But you didn't know what I wanted, did you? I could see when we were in the apartment that you wondered whether you had made the right decision, whether you would be safe with us. But had your fear been justified, it would have been too late.' He stared at her. 'Do you know what these Australian men want?'

Rachel didn't answer.

'And Rachel. Please. If you refuse to consider your own safety, then think of Gina. You have been away from her for days. You know that she was sad before you left. You should at least find out why before you decide to send her home without you.'

Rachel opened her mouth to protest, but Pravi put up his hand. 'Do you have money?'

Rachel nodded, frowning.

'And you know the name and location of your hotel?'

'Yes, of course I do,' she snapped.

'Then, there is a taxi rank outside. When you have finished your chai, go to your friend. Leave the Australian men to their own adventures.'

And with that he put two rupees on the table, got up and left.

Chapter 41 – Sandrine

The yogi said today that the truth is only one, it cannot be many. He told me of a quote: "The best things cannot be said. The second-best things cannot be understood. The third best is conversation." He said that the unified nature of the universe is such that there are connections between all things. Sounds, numbers, architectural design, mathematical principles, that all reveal to us the divine oneness in all things.

Brahma is a cube; Shiva is a string. The string vibrates. Inner energy spins around an axis and vibrates at a particular rate. This is the dance of Shiva. Our goal is to reach the absolute vibration – the divine vibration. The universe exists between the nights of Brahma. The play of consciousness is the dance of Shiva. A sphere is the final form of energy. The Shiva Lingam is the first symbol of God. In him we live, move and have our being. Attachment is a barrier, which emanates from the ego alone.

I think I begin to understand that I am a singular point. I am here but I am leaving. I am becoming less and less solid. Sometimes I barely recognise myself. Last night I stared in a mirror at my face for a long time, trying to find myself there. My features were a mystery to me. I must begin to let myself go.

Chapter 42 – Rachel

Pravi's words accompanied Rachel in the taxi, fuelling her indignation. What gave this man the right to lecture her? After he left, Rachel felt so incensed, so insulted, that she just sat and stared. Of course, he wasn't right, she told herself. But even so, she fished her mobile phone out of her backpack. It had just enough battery left, and she called Gina. But Gina didn't answer; the phone rang and rang until it went to voicemail. Rachel hung up and tried again. Voicemail again. She didn't leave a message, reasoning that Gina was obviously off somewhere enjoying herself. Rachel was pleased. This proved Pravi wrong.

As the taxi left the station and followed the curve of the road towards Kanyakumari, she looked out at the busy street and wondered whether Pravi had gone home, what he would tell his friends, his parents. Rachel knew that he had told his parents that he was going with a group of friends to Mumbai, and she had thought at the time how strange this was for a man in his late twenties. But she had realised that this wasn't strange here at all; it was what his culture demanded. Even so, she now felt him to be weak. She wanted to hate him.

When the taxi approached the roundabout, Rachel leaned forward and hesitated. She could tell the driver to turn right and take her back to their hotel, or he could take her straight into the centre of town. She stared at the back of the driver's head, noted his oily hair sticking to his big, wrinkled neck. He smelled of incense and sweat. What was the point of going to the hotel, she thought? Gina isn't there anyhow. She leaned forward and told the driver to go straight ahead.

The taxi stopped close to Bagavathi Amman Temple, and Rachel walked the short distance to the bar. It was hot and crowded in the town centre, and as it was only half past five Rachel decided to wait for Marcus and the others at the bar. As she pushed her way through the throng, she thought of Pravi, but as anger bit her again, forced him out of her mind, more determined than ever to enjoy the rest of the evening. As two young women in gaily coloured saris laughed past her, she wondered what Gina was doing, but her anger towards her made her look forward savagely to seeing her new friends. She didn't have to wait; the Australians were in the bar already, sitting on the balcony upstairs, their half-drunk bottles of beer on the wooden table in front of them.

'Hey, hey, hey,' Marcus called down when he saw her.

'Look who it is, guys, it's our Rache!'

Our Rache. She liked it; it made her feel part of them.

'Hey babe, you okay? You look like ya needa drink,' Marcus said as she walked from the stairs to the table.

'You know, Marcus, I'd love a drink,' she said.'

Marcus waved the bartender over and ordered a beer for Rachel, more for everyone else.

'So, whaddid ya boyfriend want?' Paul laughed the words out. 'Tryin ta put ya off us, was he? Said we're three bad lads did he?'

The three men laughed. Rachel smiled hesitantly.

'Forgeddim, babe,' Marcus soothed. 'You're with us now.'

Rachel suddenly grabbed Marcus' bottle and swigged a big gulp of beer, relaxing as it hit her stomach. She watched herself from the outside and liked what she saw – a free-spirited and independent young woman in a bar in India with a group of carefree Australian backpackers. Marcus winked at her. When the beers arrived, Rachel held her bottle up in front of her.

'To us,' she said brightly. 'And to all of India!'

'To us!' the Australians chorused. And they clinked their beer bottles together.

By seven o'clock the group were raucous, drunk and hungry, and they decided to go off and get something to eat. Rachel phoned Gina again, much prompted by the Australians, who thought that she should come and join them. When Gina still didn't answer, the Australians laughed.

'She's dumped ya, man!' Ben snorted. 'She's having a good time without ya!'

Rachel supposed she was and wondered tetchily whether Gina was deliberately not answering her phone in order to make a point.

They found a beachfront restaurant, and the four of them sat outside under a thatched roof, which provided dappled shade and some relief from the still-fierce heat. One of the Australians said they had to keep their strength up, and another said that all this curry would go straight through them so they had better be careful what they ate. So Rachel ordered fried chicken and chips along with the men, and they drank more beers before ordering glasses of honeybee brandy.

'Rache, are you serious about coming with us?'

They were drinking the brandy and Rachel was more than a little drunk. Marcus was looking straight at her with a strange, intense look, the set of his mouth, a slight furrow of his brow making him look forceful.

'Hell, yes!' she said, in a voice that Rachel hoped sounded light and fun, at the same time wondering why she was speaking like this. The brandy was making her feel heavy, and she didn't want to spoil the mood.

'We'll be here a few days, I should think,' Marcus said. 'Bum around, spend a bit of time on the beach. Then we'll head up. Don't wanna really kick back just yet. We only just got here, and anyhow Tamil Nadu will be chill.'

Rachel listened to Marcus' vernacular and pushed away the thought that it was beginning to irritate her. 'Yeah fine, suits me,' she said. 'You have my number, just let me know when we're leaving.'

By the time they had finished their meal and drinks it was almost dark. The sky was streaked with red and Rachel pointed this out to the Australians. She thought it looked like blood smeared across the sky, but she didn't say so. She was feeling light-headed and elated again. Stuff you, Gina, she thought. She wasn't going to let her sulking spoil her fun. And stuff Pravi too. She suggested that they go back to Dreams and finish off the night with cocktails. The Australians thought this an excellent plan, and they weaved boisterously through the streets, pushing and calling to each other, their words crashing together, held in concert by their raucous laughter.

Back at Dreams, Rachel drank Uraak and Limca and forced herself to laugh uproariously when she got hiccups. Marcus draped his arm around her shoulder and laughed along with her. Rachel stiffened for a second but didn't move away. After her second cocktail, Marcus told Ben and Paul that he and Rachel were going for a walk and that they'd see the others later.

'Goodonya man,' Paul said, and Ben grinned and clapped him on the shoulder whilst nodding into his beer. Marcus picked up Rachel's backpack and steered her out of the bar and onto the hot, dark street. It was late. Rachel wasn't sure where they were going, and she felt swimmy and unsteady on her feet. He still had his arm around her.

'Marcus,' she said, 'where are we going?'

'Shhh,' he replied quietly, 'don't worry babe, you're with me now. I'll look afta ya.'

'Wait,' Rachel said. She felt hollow and nauseous. 'Wait, I'm not going back to your hostel with you. I have to get back.'

'Rache, come on. Don't worry about your friend. She's out doing her own thing.'

'No, Marcus, I have to get back, honestly I do.'

She extricated herself unsteadily from his arm.

'Hey babe, come on, don't you trust me?'

He sounded hurt.

'Listen, Marcus.' She summoned what she hoped was an organised tone. 'I need to get back. Gina will be expecting me.' She held out her hand for her backpack.

'Come on, Rache, it's early yet. Tell ya what, come for one last drink then, a nightcap. We'll go back to the bar.'

But Rachel was taking her pack from Marcus' shoulder, hoisting it with some difficulty onto her own. 'No, I'm going to go back. But look, call me tomorrow. We'll meet up. I'll bring Gina too, I promise.'

Rachel had spotted a taxi, and before Marcus could answer she stumbled over to it and opened the door, stuffing the backpack in before tumbling in herself. Once inside she wound down the window. 'Call me,' she said. 'Call me tomorrow.'

Chapter 43 – Sandrine

Yesterday I had an impression that the place that we go to when we meditate is like a secret room and that it is possible to step right into it. I had the sense that it is possible to view our waking world as a kind of a screen whereby we can watch a fiction, which at times might be entertaining or moving or fear-inducing or any other manner of theme. But in the room there is an absence of all such distractions. In our secret room we may simply be, with no swaying towards this emotion or that distraction.

I realised that Kali is the destroyer of all that anchors us to Maya, the world of illusion. Kali is the destroyer of the ego and of all worldly attachments. This is why she appears so terrifying. If one holds on to the ego and to worldly attachments, then one will fear Kali. I realised also that this is why Christians say that we should fear God. It is a fear of losing the 'I'. Because in the great unity, there is no 'I'. It is why Christians say that we should surrender ourselves to God and put our trust in him. We must quite literally lose ourselves.

Edges. Edges are places of uncertainty, of transition, of change and creativity. Our language reflects this in phrases like 'living on the edge, 'on a knife edge', 'the edge of reason', 'edgy'. I am on the edge.

Chapter 44 – Rachel

The day broke slowly over a slumbering world. Birds greeted the newly born sunlight with their song, and monkeys chattered and screeched. The sea was restless as it hunted the shore, grabbing, running, grabbing. Rachel slept long and deep into the day without dreaming. It was the most she had slept in three fractured nights.

Rachel's waking moments were sweet and seductive yet clouded by a vague knowledge of the waking state to come. She savoured the in-between time, neither awake nor asleep, aware of rising out of the consciousness-beyond-consciousness, like arriving somewhere she didn't want to go. She pulled her blanket tightly around her and curled into a ball, taking pleasure in the warmth and comfort of her bed. She lay like that for some time before she stretched out her legs, her arms and yawned widely. Something in the air told her that it was late in the day.

Rachel realised with a jolt that Gina's bed was empty. She swung her legs out of her own bed and sat looking at Gina's. It was perfectly made, and the room boy had characteristically made a flower out of some rolled-up towels and placed it on top. Rachel stared at it. What did this mean, she wondered? Had Gina come back late last night and left again this morning? If so, then the room boy had been in to clean the room whilst Rachel was still sleeping. She supposed this was possible since it was very late – gone twelve, she discovered with a glance at her watch. It didn't seem likely though. The room boys would be more likely to creep out quietly if they saw someone still sleeping. She tried to think back to last night. Was Gina in the bed when she got in? But Rachel could barely remember arriving at all. She seemed to remember feeling glad that she wouldn't have to talk, but she might have thought this if Gina had been sleeping when she got back.

Rachel reached for her phone. The battery was flat. It hadn't been charged since before she went to Mumbai, and it was now completely dead. Rachel flung it onto the bed and went to look for her charger, which wasn't plugged into her adapter in the wall. After flinging clothes and towels around and opening and shutting drawers, she found it in a drawer in the nightstand and plugged it into the adapter and the phone into it. It would take some time before it beeped back into life.

Ok, Rachel thought, so Gina might have stayed out last night. On the other hand she might have gone out early this morning. There is no need to worry. She'll be back soon enough either way. She was expecting me yesterday so she's probably trying to make a point, to prove that she has places to go as well. Rachel couldn't deny that her worry was spiked with annoyance. She thought that Gina was being childish. She had probably met up with some people and gone off with them to teach her a lesson.

Rachel padded through to the kitchen and set about making tea. The kitchen was tidy and the bin had been emptied. This worried Rachel still further as it suggested that perhaps Gina hadn't been here since before the room boys had been yesterday morning.

She took her tea onto the balcony. The strength of the sun's heat further intensified her growing anger, and she sat and fumed and worried silently as she sipped.

For God sake, Gina, she thought, where are you? She put her cup down and went back to the bedroom to see if the phone had charged enough for it to work yet. It hadn't. Well, okay, she thought. She'd leave it until later on, and if Gina still wasn't back she would start making enquiries.

Rachel decided that she should shower and dress. The cool water felt fresh against her hot skin, and she stayed in the shower for a full twenty minutes. She watched the dirty water collecting in the tray and imagined some kind of fresh start. She thought briefly of Marcus and the others and wondered what they were doing now. She felt that familiar feeling where she didn't want to leave the shower, but preferred to stay there under the warm water, feeling calm and refreshed.

Once out and dried off, she dressed in clean trousers and a tee-shirt and brushed her damp hair back into a knot. It felt so good to be in clean clothes at last. She checked to see if her phone worked yet. It did. She immediately called Gina.

'The number you are calling is not available.'

Stupid, smug, monotone voice, Rachel thought. She decided to see if Gina had left her a message at reception.

There was no one on the path outside. Rachel supposed that most of the hotel guests would be finishing their lunch. There were one or two guests around the pool, and Rachel nodded at a fat man wearing a towel who had nodded politely at her as she passed. At the reception a man in a smart white shirt whom she didn't recognise greeted her brightly as she entered.

'Hi,' she said. 'I wonder if my friend, Gina McKenzie, has left a message for me at all? We are staying here together.'

The man consulted a book in front of him and some pigeonholes behind him. 'I am sorry, madam, there appears to be no message.'

Rachel smiled her thanks and walked out of the cool reception room. She could smell spicy cooking coming from the dining area and decided that she might as well eat lunch if it wasn't too late.

Rachel chose some samba and rice from the buffet table and sat down with a glass of water. She picked at her meal. The spices were delicious, but she found that she wasn't hungry after all and pushed her food around the plate in front of her. The other guests left in small groups and in couples. They annoyed Rachel, and she didn't smile or greet anyone, keeping her eyes on her plate. When she decided at last that she couldn't face the food, it occurred to her that she ought to get back to her room where her phone was still charging, in case Gina tried to call her. She scraped her chair back and walked self-consciously from the dining area. She hoped that the other guests didn't think that she had been stood up. She thought of Gina eating alone for the last few days. Or perhaps she hadn't eaten alone. A fresh wave of anger washed over her. As soon as she opened her door Rachel could hear the shrill ring of her mobile phone. She ran to the bedroom and caught it just in time.

'Hello Gina?' she said, breathless and impatient.

'Not unless I've had a secret sex-change I don't know about!'

Marcus. Rachel vaguely remembered telling him to phone her today.

'So whacha up ta, babe? You wanna hang out or what? We're off ta the beach.'

'I can't come,' Rachel answered. 'Gina isn't here.'

'That's no prob. Come by yerself.'

'No, I mean Gina didn't come back last night. I haven't seen her.'

'Ha ha!' he boomed. 'Guess what, guys, Rache's friend's done a runner! Prob'ly gone off with some Bruce! No worries, Rache, come to the beach with us. She can meet us there later on.'

Rachel felt strangely grateful that Marcus was so unconcerned about Gina's absence. Perhaps it meant that she was worrying unnecessarily. But even so, she felt that she ought to stay in the hotel for when Gina did return. She explained this to Marcus.

'No worries, princess. P'raps we'll meet up for a beer later, yeah? Give us a call when your friend comes back. She can come too.'

Chapter 45 – Sandrine

There is an air of excitement here. The women have dressed in colourful celebration clothes. We are performing the Durga Puga. The lamps have been brought from the temple to the large hall, and brightly coloured yantras have been painted on the floor. We have been preparing the lotus flowers and the offerings of bright-red kumkuma powder all day. It is evening and dark, but the moon is bright. Soon we will chant to her and make our offerings to the universal mother.

I realised that as the moon waxes and wanes so our energy focuses inward and out. Last week I was very introspective. Now I have moved out. We must be continually aware of what we have learned and find ways to live it. Gandhi said, 'Be the change you want to see.' Learning must change us – otherwise it isn't learning at all. The yogi told me that constantly thinking of a person or a thing has the effect of creating an attachment to it and that if we are to rid ourselves of worldly attachments then we must actively seek to remove this person or this thing from our thoughts. I am not my body or my name. My dharma is to shed the attachments to these things. This is the dharma of all of us. We are all live dead bodies.

Perelle, I have not written of you for some time. I have sought to push you from my thoughts since I know now that you stand in the way of my continuing inner-journey. I must detach from you. Indeed to some extent now, I do stand detached from you. Not because of your silence but in pursuit of my own. The things of the ego must be severed. I must bid them goodbye, and they must be left to their own Karma. You and I shared a journey together; we walked for a while on the same path. We must have had something to teach each other. But now our paths must diverge and we must go separately into our further karma. You are a mandala drawn in the sand, beautiful and intricate. But over time the wind blows the grains of sand away and the pattern shifts and fades until it is no longer there at all. Perelle, I am no longer your Sandrine.

Chapter 46 – Rachel

It was nearly six o'clock and Gina still wasn't back. Rachel had been phoning her number all afternoon. She had jumped up each time she heard someone outside, wishing and wishing for it to be Gina, but each time she had been disappointed. She sat on the balcony and watched the happy holidaymakers going about their carefree day, laughing and smiling and chatting as though nothing in the world was wrong. She couldn't comprehend how they could be so unaffected whilst she was so scared. Her anger had fuelled an inner remonstrating, and she had played through all sorts of outbursts in her head, practising what she would say to Gina when finally she saw her coming through the front gate and up the red path to their rooms. But each time she looked up Gina wasn't there, and eventually the anger began to mutate into a sticky, nagging doubt.

She tried to read, but she couldn't concentrate and kept coming back again and again to the question of where Gina was. She began to wonder if she ought to phone home, to Richard perhaps, or Gina's parents. But what could she say to them? And in any case, what could they do? Besides she wasn't sure she should worry them yet.

Eventually she decided that she would have to raise the alarm and she went once more to the reception and asked to speak with the manager. The manager, a large, jovial-looking man with a shiny bald head led Rachel through to a dark back office where a noisy fan tried to stir the thick air. Rachel wasn't sure how to start but managed eventually to explain her predicament to the man.

He looked at her doubtfully. 'So, you went to Mumbai and when you returned your friend was not here?'

It sounded rather lame when put like that, but Rachel confirmed that this was the case and said again that she didn't think that Gina had come back to the room last night.

'And you fully expected that she would be here on your return?'

'Of course,' Rachel answered, slightly irritated by the question.

'Where do think your friend might be?'

Rachel answered that she didn't know.

'Well,' the man said, 'in the first instance I think we should check the hotel and the beach. You have done this?'

Rachel said that no, she hadn't, she had stayed close to her room in case Gina returned or telephoned.

'I suggest that for now you go back to your room and continue to wait for your friend,' he said somewhat dismissively, Rachel thought. 'I am sure that she will return anytime now, but in the meantime I will discuss the situation with my security man and stay in contact with you.'

Rachel tried to say something else, but the man stood up and indicated with his outstretched arm and a cursory nod of his head that she should leave.

Rachel hurried back to their room, not wanting to see any of the other hotel guests. She waited. No one came. She called Gina's number again. Still no connection. She made herself some tea but didn't drink it. She wandered out onto the balcony and stood looking down the red path and the other way towards the car park, willing Gina to appear. Her hands were pressed together, and she was tapping the tips of her fingers against her lips. What was the manager doing, she wondered? Time passed. Her phone rang and Rachel jumped, but the display told her that it was Marcus again. She let it ring without answering. Rachel decided to go back and talk to manager once more, to see what he had done.

It didn't appear as though the manager had done anything. In his office once more, he put down his coffee cup, folded his newspaper and indicated with a nod of his head that Rachel should sit. He seemed irritated that she had come back.

'Yes, miss, what can I do for you now?' he said.

'My friend still hasn't come back, and I am really worried now,' Rachel said in a small voice.

The manager sighed and picked up the receiver of the old-fashioned telephone on his desk and spoke quickly into it in Tamil. A few moments later a security guard came into the office. He didn't sit down.

'If you would give us a description of your friend, my colleague here will instigate a search.'

The manager sounded impatient. Rachel wondered what they would be searching for. Gina hiding in the cleaner's cupboard or behind the bar? She suppressed a laugh that would have bordered on hysteria. But she co-operated and told the men what Gina looked like, what she was likely to be wearing, described her new red bag. She felt that at least she was taking some kind of action.

'Do you think you should call the police?' Rachel asked. She felt frightened now. The fact that they were searching for Gina intensified the fact that she was missing.

186

'No, miss, I do not think it would be appropriate to involve the police in this matter at present.' He stood and once again indicated that she should do the same. 'Please, stay within the confines of the hotel and we will deal with matters. She winced. Gina was now a 'matter'.

Rachel thought of phoning Pravi. She didn't want to, but it was now almost seven o'clock and it was getting dark. In her room once more she picked up her phone and called him. He answered at once, his voice dark and sweet.

'Pravi.' Rachel was sobbing, she couldn't get her words out.

'What has happened, Rachel. Are you okay?'

'No,' she replied. 'Gina isn't here. She didn't come back last night, and I don't know where she is.'

'Where are you?'

'I'm in the hotel.'

'Don't go anywhere. I'll come straight over.'

Rachel was so relieved that she continued to cry quietly. She didn't know what Pravi could do, but if she had to talk to the police he would know what to do. Pravi was her only connection to the place, the people, the customs. She felt a hollow sense of how possible it was to feel so alone, so completely unconnected. She realised how vulnerable this made her. Knowing that Pravi was on his way, she felt grateful and guilty.

Pravi arrived within half an hour, and they sat in the little living-area while Rachel told him what had happened.

'You are sure that Gina was not here last night?' he asked.

'Well, no I'm not sure at all. I got back late. I'd been drinking. With the Australians.'

Rachel looked down. She hadn't wanted to tell Pravi this part of the story, and she felt grateful when he didn't respond.

'Let me make some calls,' Pravi said.

Rachel sat in silence while he phoned those of his friends who had met Gina. He spoke in Tamil, but Rachel could tell from his face that none of those he spoke with had seen her. Eventually Pravi put his mobile phone into his pocket. 'Have you spoken to the hotel manager?' he asked quietly.

'Yes, twice,' Rachel answered, 'but I haven't heard anything since I last spoke to him and the security guard over an hour ago.'

'I am not surprised,' Pravi replied. 'The hotel management won't want to upset the other guests and certainly won't want the involvement of the police.' They would, he said, in all likelihood deal with the situation in a cursory manner in the hope that Gina would return of her own accord.

'You stay here. I will go and speak with the manager myself.'

He left the room. Rachel sat back on the small couch and crossed her legs under her. She felt a faint but welcome sense of relief; something was being done at last.

Pravi returned ten minutes later. 'It is as I thought,' he said. 'The hotel manager is unwilling at this stage to do anything at all. He says that if Gina hasn't returned by tomorrow morning he will call the police.'

'Tomorrow morning?' Rachel was beside herself. 'That's far too long to wait. Anything could have happened!'

'Come with me,' Pravi said.

Rachel trailed after Pravi to the bar. Guests were gathering for the evening's eating and drinking. Some were already sitting at tables in the dining area. Pravi spoke quietly to the bartender. He said something to Pravi and went through a door behind the bar, coming back moments later with another man. Pravi spoke to him and he looked at Rachel and nodded, speaking quietly to Pravi.

'What did he say?' Rachel asked as Pravi led them to the beach path.

'The other man was on duty yesterday and the day before. He said that he recognised you as Gina's friend and that Gina was in the hotel two days ago, that she sat by the pool by herself. He had wondered why she was alone.'

Rachel wondered if there was a note of reproach in Pravi's voice.

'He says that Gina went to the beach in the afternoon but that he hasn't seen her at the hotel since.'

They hurried along the beach path, past the thatched shops and the massage shack. Everything was closed and dark. No one was on the beach. The sand stretched down towards the dark sea. Rachel shivered although it was still very warm. They stumbled along the sand to the shack where a few couples were sitting at tables drinking and talking quietly. Hindi music was playing in the background.

'Wait here,' Pravi said and went to speak with the man behind the bar. Rachel saw the man look over in her direction and shake his head. Pravi said something else, appearing to be rather more insistent. The barman looked at Rachel again. They spoke for a few moments more, the man shaking his head once or twice. Pravi said something else and took his hand out of his pocket, laying it on the bar. Did Rachel see money change hands? She wasn't sure. The man went into his shack and was gone for some moments. Pravi waited at the bar without turning around, and when the man returned Rachel saw that he was carrying a red bag. Pravi took the bag and brought it over to Rachel.

'That's Gina's bag!' she exclaimed. The little mirrors looked dull and dead.

'The guy says that a girl left it here and went off up the beach in the direction of Kanyakumari. They thought she was coming back, so they kept the bag for her, but she didn't return. The man said he thought he recognised you as her friend.'

Rachel looked inside the bag. There were a few of Gina's things there. Rachel recognised her hairbrush, a cigarette lighter. There was no phone and no purse. What could it mean?

'I suspect that Gina's phone and purse were in the bag when she left it,' Pravi said, flicking a glance at the barman, who was polishing a glass and looking sideways at Pravi and Rachel.

Rachel stared up and down the dark beach. She thought of Gina on the beach that other night, how she had been lying on the sand, tears in her eyes, how she had cried. Why, she thought, did she leave Gina here? It was so clear to her now that something had been wrong. She thought of Pravi in the café by the station, quietly imploring her to go back to Gina, and her insistence on meeting the Australians, the stupid Australians who couldn't give a stuff about Gina.

Rachel looked at him. 'Pravi,' she stammered. There were tears in her eyes.

Pravi hugged her briefly but tightly. 'Come,' he said.

'Where to?' Rachel asked, wiping her face.

'We will go back to your room and decide what we can do.'

Chapter 47 – Sandrine

I am sitting in the large hall at the ashram. Some Indian women are chanting in one corner. Two more women are laughing together as they spread rush mats out on the floor. People are gathering and sitting around the edges of the hall. The women are setting out tambourines and drums, and someone is ringing a bell. A man has begun to play a tabla. More people are assembling and moving their mats to the centre of the hall. It is almost dark.

I am preparing for a departure. I am preparing to leave, in the truest sense of the word. I am almost ready. There are some final preparations to make before I can leave myself and arrive at a blissful union. I have fully entered my silence now, and slowly the attachments of the world have slipped away. I am an old woman facing death. I am a baby facing birth. In all that is pure, all that is free, all that is eternal, I surrender to this, fully and completely.

I find that the people around me are slipping away. More and more I see that they are fascinating but nothing more. I begin to see who they truly are, and the projections of their egos and my own mean less and less to me. I know now who Perelle is. He is an eternal soul as am I, as are all of us. I thank him, and I bid him well on his journey. Our fellow travellers will slip away once they have given us our gift and we have given them theirs. One day there will be no more fellow-travellers as we will have no further need for their gifts, but at that point we won't be alone. We are only alone when we need others around us to help us to work towards our dharma. We are only alone when we connect with our ego to worldly things and people, which we mistake for reality, but which are in fact Maya.

Chapter 48 – Rachel

Back in the room, Pravi made tea for Rachel and made her drink it. He added lots of sugar.

'You must keep your strength,' he said, setting the cup down on the table in front of her. 'Have you eaten anything today?'

'I tried to eat at lunchtime, but I couldn't,' Rachel answered.

Pravi found some biscuits in the kitchen. 'Starving yourself will not help Gina,' he said, handing her one.

Rachel didn't want anything, but she ate a biscuit to please him. She held onto Gina's red bag, hugging it tightly to her chest. 'Why would Gina go off without her bag?' she said. 'Why would she leave it at the shack without going back for it?'

Pravi didn't answer.

'Do you think,' she asked, 'that Gina might just have forgotten her bag and the shack-people stole it before she came back for it? Maybe she did come back, but it wasn't there?'

'I doubt that,' Pravi answered. 'The shack-guys rely on business from the hotels. They wouldn't want to get a bad reputation. My guess would be that they held onto the bag and took Gina's money and phone from it only when it was clear that Gina wasn't coming back.'

'That explains why Gina's phone won't connect,' Rachel said.

'Yes, whoever has the phone now will certainly have changed the SIM card.'

'Maybe Gina is safe somewhere but can't get in touch, then. Especially since she doesn't have her purse.'

But Rachel could think of no reason why Gina wouldn't have left a message before setting out to wherever she had gone. It all pointed to the terrible possibility that Gina couldn't get in touch. They talked about going to the police. Pravi was doubtful that they would be interested since there was no apparent crime.

'They might be more interested if Gina had been missing for a number of days,' he said.

'For all we know,' Rachel answered, 'she has been missing since the day we left for Mumbai.'

'That isn't the case, Rachel. Remember that the hotel barman saw her by the pool the day before yesterday.' He looked hard at Rachel. 'The police might become more interested if they were bribed,' he said.

Rachel looked at him in alarm. He wasn't joking.

'Rachel,' Pravi said quietly. 'The police can be our last option, and we can bribe them if we need to.'

Rachel stared at him, eyes wide with fear.

'But before we go down that route, is there anyone, anyone at all that you can think of, who might have had some contact with Gina, who might know something?'

Rachel thought of the shack-men from their night on the beach. She thought of friends of Pravi's, but he had already phoned. She told Pravi that the only other person she could think of was Sarada.

'But I doubt she'd be with her,' Rachel said. 'We've only met her a few times. She's just a woman with a juice shack.'

'Where is this shack?' Pravi asked.

'It is quite a way along the beach on the way to Kanyakumari.'

'Well, that is the direction that she went,' he said. 'Do you have any contact details for this Sarada?'

'All I know is that she lives in the shack and looks after a man's apartment sometimes,' Rachel replied. 'I know where the shack is, but I'm not sure she will be able to help us.'

'Come on,' said Pravi. 'It's worth a try.'

They ran down the steps and out of the hotel gate. The security guard looked at them disapprovingly, Rachel thought, as she climbed onto the back of Pravi's bike. As they sped through the dark streets past holiday revellers and late-night shopkeepers and onto the open road, Rachel couldn't help thinking about how excited she had felt the last time she was on the back of Pravi's bike. The feel of his body in front of her, the speed and the thrill of the ride, the freedom and frisson had made her want to shout. Once again neither of them wore a helmet, but this time it didn't seem so funny when Pravi stopped at the bridge to put his on.

'I have to Rachel,' Pravi said when Shecomplained that he was slowing them down. 'The police will stop us if I don't wear a helmet on the bridge road, and that would slow us down even more.'

At the shack all was dark, and it was clear that no one was there.

'It's closed,' Rachel said, rattling the wood-and-thatch door.

'Sarada,' she called. No one answered. Pravi looked around. The place was deserted. There weren't even any holidaymakers around.

'Rachel, you said that she looks after an apartment sometimes.'

Rachel nodded.

'Do you know where it is?'

'I don't know the actual address. I think the man who lives there said past the harbour.'

'Was the man Indian?' Pravi asked.

'No, American I think. Why?'

'Well,' said Pravi, 'there are lots of apartment blocks there, but a foreigner is probably more likely to have one of the beachfront ones. Would you recognise it if you saw it?'

'No, I've never been there.' Rachel frowned at Pravi. 'But is there much point? Why would she be there?'

'Anything is worth a try,' answered Pravi.

'I'd recognise his car,' she said suddenly. 'It's some kind of blue jeep with no roof.'

It took them half an hour to get to Kanyakumari. Pravi drove as fast as he dared, hooting and weaving between traffic, pedestrians and cows. The streets in the town were alive with people, and Rachel wondered if she would catch a glimpse of the Australians coming out of some bar. She hoped not. They drove at speed along the beach road, hooting and swaying with the rest of the traffic. They passed an enormous sign, which read 'Luxury Lavatory', and Rachel remembered joking with Gina the first time they'd seen it about what could be so luxurious about it. They passed the café where she and Gina had drunk cappuccino before trying to book tickets to the tiger sanctuary, and Rachel thought of the other café in Mumbai where she and Pravi had met Vish. How long ago that seemed.

They passed the giant statue of Thiruvalluvar, dramatically floodlit on it's little island, the sea dark and restless around it.

'Can you go any faster?' Rachel shouted as they swerved past a lumbering cow.

Pravi didn't answer. Soon they began to leave the main town behind and came to a line of street vendors selling snack foods in a wide pavement. The area was crowded. It seemed to be a place where young people congregated, and Pravi had to slow down as bikes and scooters came and went and more people arrived and left. As they continued further, Rachel began to look intently at the apartment buildings. Pravi slowed down.

'It must be along here somewhere,' he shouted. Rachel stared into the car-parking areas in front of the buildings as they passed. All she saw were white Muratis and mopeds.

'I don't see it,' she shouted over the noise of the traffic.

'Keep looking,' Pravi shouted back. They continued along the beach road, Pravi slowing by each apartment block. On they drove, mopeds and taxis swerving past them as Rachel twisted around as far as she could on the back of the bike, scanning the forecourts and the pavements.

'It's no use...' she started to say when suddenly she saw it, Sarada's friend's blue jeep in the car park of a big white block.

'There!' she shouted, and Pravi braked and turned abruptly, a cacophony of angry hooting, and crunched to a halt amid a cloud of dust rising around them.

They got off the bike and stood looking at the blue jeep.

'That's definitely his car,' Rachel said. They looked up at the building. It seemed to be perhaps eight storeys high, with balconies facing the sea.

'You've no idea which one?' said Pravi.

'None,' Rachel replied.

They entered the lobby and went up a flight of stairs. There was no night-watchman to ask. None of the doors had a name plate, and in any case Rachel couldn't remember the name of Sarada's friend if she'd ever been told it. She looked at Pravi, who gestured towards the first door with a nod of his head and knocked. They waited. Rachel realised she was holding her breath and began exhaling slowly. No answer. Pravi turned and knocked on the second door.

After a moment a middle-aged woman opened the door. She was wearing a pretty pink salwar kameez, and Rachel could hear the sound of a television coming from inside the flat, could smell spicy cooking. Pravi said something to the woman in Tamil, and Rachel made out the words 'American' and the name 'Sarada'. A man's voice called from inside the flat and the woman turned and called something back. Then she nodded at Pravi – the sideways nod that Rachel had seen so often here – and said something, smiling and pointing up the stairway. Rachel felt her heart race as Pravi told her what the woman had said.

'Fourth floor, number forty-three,' said Pravi.

'Thank you so much,' Rachel said to the woman, not sure if she would understand, and without waiting for an answer she raced ahead of Pravi up the stairs to the fourth floor. Outside number forty-three Rachel rapped the knocker three times in quick succession, unable to contain her nervous apprehension. The door opened almost immediately. It was Sarada.

Chapter 49 – Sandrine

Kanyakumari, place of the virgin mother. There on the beach at sunset I burned my clothes, and I stood there by the sea, naked and exposed.

On the beach there was a shell. The tide gave it to me, and my heart recognised it. I had been looking for it, but without knowing it, and when I saw it something powerful was conceived and started to grow inside me.

I knelt by the smoking fire and intoned the words I'd been taught. 'May the goddess Saraswati, who wears a garland, white like the kunda flower, the moon and the snow, who is adorned with pure-white clothes, whose hands are ornamented with veena and the gesture of blessings, who is seated on a white lotus, who is always worshipped by Brahama, Vishnu, Shiva and other gods, who is the remover of all inertness and lifelessness, protect me.'

I stood. I stared at what remained of my burning clothes. I put on a white robe and knew that I no longer had a name, that Sandrine had left me and that I had no past and no future. I picked up the shell.

Chapter 50 – Rachel

Before Rachel could speak, Sarada turned and gestured for her and Pravi to come in. 'Thank God,' was all she said.

Pravi and Rachel hurried into the lounge after Sarada and sat down on the sofa at Sarada's bidding.

She sat on another sofa. The apartment was quiet and dimly lit. Sarada indicated that Rachel and Pravi should stay quiet by bringing her finger to her lips.

'What's going on Sarada? Is Gina here? She hasn't been back to hotel in two days.'

Rachel's fear was making her gabble, but she didn't care. Sarada sat forward, her elbows on her knees. She leant further forward, clasped her hands in front of her. 'Rachel,' Sarada said quietly. 'Gina is here.'

'Oh thank God, thank God,' cried Rachel, a sob catching in her throat.

'But listen to me,' Sarada put up her hand. 'Something has happened, and I don't know what. Gina is in a terrible state. She hasn't spoken a word since I brought her here two days ago.'

'Gina.' Her voice was a whisper. 'Gina, it's me Rachel.'

She sat on the edge of the bed. The room was dark and Gina was curled into a tight ball under the cover. Rachel laid her hand on Gina's shoulder, and Gina flinched. She looked terrible, her eyes crusted and face burnt a deep and painful red. She looked at Rachel.

'Gina, it's me,' Rachel said again. She was crying, the tears running silently down her face.

Gina struggled to sit. Her eyes were ringed with dark shadows. 'Rachel,' she whispered.'

Now they sat on the balcony of the apartment. It was warm and so quiet they couldn't even hear the sea. A wind chime tinkled prettily in the almost imperceptible breeze. They sat in silence for a long time, two cups of tea on the glass table in front of them. Sarada had suggested quietly to Pravi that they leave the two women alone and go out to have chai at a nearby café. They had left, quietly closing the door behind them, and Rachel watched as the blue jeep pulled out of the car park and disappeared down the road.

'Gina,' she said eventually, hesitantly. 'Gina, I am so, so sorry.'

Gina picked up her tea. She blew it gently although it wasn't hot anymore.

'Rachel,' she said, staring into the tea. She took a deep breath. 'There's something I have to tell you.'

Chapter 51 – Sandrine

I sat by the sea all night with the shell in my hand. There were clouds in the sky, but they did not obscure the moonlight. The shore expanded to my left and to my right. Above the drone of the waves I could hear chanting and drumming from the temple. The moon was restless in the water. I could see stars between the clouds.

'If we worship her as the great mother, she will, through her benign grace and blessings, remove all obstacles in the path and lead us safely into the unlimited domain of eternal bliss. Only then will we be absolutely free.'

A bell rang in the temple. A lone bird flew across the ocean and disappeared into the darkness.

I heard a baby crying from a long way away. I knew that it was time to throw the shell into the water.

Chapter 52 – Gina

The sun glared down as Gina stood by the shore staring out at the distended sea as it pushed the crashing waves towards her, her upturned palm still holding the shell.

On the same beach, in the darkness and heat of the night, a man had asked, 'Where your baby?'

The question leapt at Gina. She looked at the little dog sleeping in her lap. She looked up at the men sitting with her on the sunloungers.

'I'm sorry,' she said. 'I'm a little drunk. Could you repeat more slowly please?'

'You mother. Your baby?'

She stared at the man. 'I'm sorry,' she repeated, frowning. 'I don't quite understand what you are saying. What do you mean?'

'Baby,' he said. 'Your baby.' He was quietly insistent.

'I… What do you mean, my baby?' Gina looked from one man to another. They were all looking at her.

'Your baby not with you. You without baby,' he repeated.

'No… my… my baby isn't with me…' She spoke slowly, carefully. An appalling apprehension of what they were saying kicked her in the stomach and she almost gagged.

'No baby here,' one of the men said. Her head started to buzz. Something was ringing behind her eyes, and they felt hot and heavy in their sockets. Vomit rose in her throat. She fought it, staring from one brown face to another.

'Why?' one of them asked. 'In India, mother with baby.' His eyebrows were raised.

'Yes, but…'

'In India, this sacred bond. Mother and baby. Mother is above all. She is like goddess. She has power of life and death.'

'Why are you saying this?' Her words were desperate, pleading.

'It is strange for us, that is all. When you mother, then your obligation is to baby. Your baby not with you. We try to understand, is all.'

'I have no baby. I am not a mother. I am not a mother!'

'Why you angry? You maybe sad because you not with baby? You miss baby?'

'No! I don't miss the baby! Please! Leave me alone, just leave me alone.' She choked on her tears and vomited onto the sand. She stood up, stumbling, and looked wildly around for Rachel, pushing away a man who was trying to steady her.

'Okay, okay, you quiet now. Please, you sit down. Please. We find your friend.'

Now, in the apartment on the quiet balcony she spoke the words.

'Rachel,' she said. 'I've had an abortion.'

The significance of the barren word, the weight of it, came crashing into the sentence. She spoke now to Rachel, quietly, staring out over the balcony towards the dark sea beyond.

'I knew it was too soon for me to have a baby. Richard and I talked endlessly about it, we considered all the options, but I knew I wasn't ready. I didn't think either of us was ready. The moment I saw the colour of that damn pregnancy-tester change from white to pink, I already knew my decision. I had the operation the week before we flew out here. I know, I know, it was stupid.' Gina choked on her words.

'It's okay,' Rachel said softly.

'Richard begged me not to go; he wanted to look after me, to be together, to talk. But I thought, since I was so adamant that I didn't want the baby, that I would be fine. It didn't turn out like that.

'Rachel, I wanted to tell you what had happened, but I couldn't. You were so excited about the trip, I didn't want to spoil it. I thought about telling you on the plane, but all I could think about was how all my hormones, my cells, my entire body wanted this baby, but that it wasn't there anymore. I was just so utterly overwhelmed with what I'd done.

'I started to have this awful recurring dream about a little boy on a beach and how I drowned him.' Gina closed her eyes and bit her bottom lip.

'It's okay Gina,' Rachel whispered again. 'I'm here now.' She put her hand over Gina's which were clenched together in her lap.

Gina was sitting very straight. It hurt her to move as her sunburn was so raw. She looked up at Rachel. 'When I woke up and saw you sitting there, I just wanted to cry. Rachel, I didn't know what to do, I just didn't know what to do.'

She paused, still staring out to sea. Rachel sat quietly, holding her hand.

'I went to the beach and I just stood there, looking at the sea. I think I just shut down. I stood there, not thinking about anything, I don't know for how long. It was as though the people on the beach, the waves, the sun, everything was all a part of some other world and not one that I had to bother with anymore. I don't know why, but the only thing that made any sense was a shell I picked up. I held on to it as though it were a matter of life or death.

'I suppose I must have started walking at some point. I remember the feel of the sand on my feet and the sun burning me, but somehow those things didn't seem to have anything to do with me. I don't know how long I walked for or where I was going. It didn't seem to matter.'

'Gina?' A voice reached her. 'Gina! It's me Sarada!' My god, Gina! Stop!'

Gina stopped. She looked at her. There were no words.

'Gina you look terrible! What have you done?'

Gina clutched the shell.

'Please, talk to me. What is wrong? Has something happened?'

Silence.

'Gina come with me. Come and sit down.'

She sat.

'You are red raw. Aren't you wearing any sun cream? It's forty degrees, for god's sake! Hey, over here, can we have some water please? This woman is dehydrated. She has sunstroke.'

Sarada had made her drink the water in small sips. She spoke words, many more words. She seemed to expect words back, but Gina had none to give. Sarada wanted to know about her hotel. About Rachel. She thought that maybe she had some words, but they felt like spikes, and they stuck in her throat and hurt her. Maybe they weren't words at all. Sarada wanted her to go with her. Along a street, into a big, blue car with no roof. She wanted to put a shawl around her, over her head. Gina stared out of the window at passing streets, people. It was getting dark. She remembered thinking how it was so strange that the sun came and the sun went.

In the apartment Sarada sat her on a couch, made her drink more water, but slowly. It tasted funny. Sugar. Salt. More questions. Hotel. Phone numbers. She had no answers. She sat sipping water until Sarada had finally led her to a bed and let her sleep.

Chapter 53 – Rachel

Gina had been speaking for a long time. Rachel didn't interrupt but clutched her hand tightly. Sarada had explained that she didn't remember or perhaps had never known the name of their hotel, and since Gina didn't have her phone, Sarada had no way of contacting her. Gina either wouldn't or couldn't speak, but other than sunstroke didn't appear injured in any way, so Sarada had felt it best to simply take care of her for now.

Rachel thought now about the conversation she'd had in the café in Mumbai where Pravi had said that he had told the men from the shack that Gina had a child. He had done this so that they would respect her, look after her. And in order to make polite conversation they had asked Gina about her baby, why her child wasn't on holiday with her. Rachel couldn't begin to comprehend the complex, contradictory emotions that Gina must have been going through. She thought about her irritable impatience with Gina that night, her sense of martyred self-justification at having to help Gina home. And she thought of how she had left Gina sleeping when she left for Mumbai, how she had decided to put Gina out of her mind. She thought with shame how she had planned on going off with the Australians, leaving Gina to go home alone. She hoped never to see Marcus, Paul and Ben again. She looked at Gina, saw how bravely she was trying to cope with this conversation.

'I am a selfish person,' she said.

'Rachel,' Gina replied, 'you couldn't possibly have known what I was upset about.'

'No,' said Rachel. 'But I could have asked.'

The two women sat in silence on the dark balcony, the sea spreading away from them in a black arc.

'Rachel,' said Gina quietly. 'I should have told you about the abortion before we came to India.'

Rachel nodded.

'It was irresponsible of me not to. I've placed an impossible burden on you and perhaps on Richard as well. I didn't want to spoil the trip, and I really thought that I could come to terms with this on my own. I can't. I should have told you.'

She was staring out at the sea.

'I have been angry with you, it's true, but I know that you wouldn't have left me if I'd told you what had happened.'

Rachel nodded again. 'We both should have done things differently,' she said. 'I think perhaps I need to learn to get in a little deeper. Perhaps I... sort of... leave people behind sometimes.'

'Yes,' said Gina, 'I think you do a bit.'

Rachel continued to stare ahead. 'Well, I'm here now,' she said, turning away from the sea to face Gina. She took Gina's two hands once more in her own. 'I'm really here,' she repeated. 'I don't know what I can do, but I can listen. I can care.'

Her tears were hot and wet on her face, and her jaw was aching from trying not to cry. She saw that Gina's eyes were welling with tears as well, and she leant forward and embraced her.

'Gina. Rachel.'

Both women turned around. Neither had heard Sarada coming back into the apartment. She spoke quietly.

'Will you trust me if I ask you both to do something with me? Will you come with me to the beach?'

Epilogue – Sarada

This is my point of departure. I am standing by an open door. There is a path behind me. It winds back through the years of my life, past people and places, past loves and losses, past all that I have been. The path, and all that is on it, is beginning to darken and to fade. I see Mama, far behind. She is smiling at me from the early grave that her karma took her to. I smile back. I see Papa. He too has his karma, I remind myself, as I have mine. I nod to him and he nods back.

And there is Perelle, at every step and stage of the way: beautiful, tormented Perelle, the very heart and soul of my journey here, my twin star, my home, myself. I bring my hands together and bow my head in salutation to him. I am saying a final goodbye, my brother. I do not feel sadness or loss. I know that I am all of this but none of it. The path spirals back through time, back past my birth, past my deaths, my lives, my many births, back to the centre, the source, the divine absolute. And here and now, at the threshold, at the door, I am again at the core. My stories have ended, have come to their final conclusions, and I stand ready to follow Kali through the destruction of all worldly attachments, all that I once held dear, all that I thought defined me, into my final departure.

The women lit candles and adorned me with flowers. They gave me fruits and almonds. They hugged me and chanted '*aum tryambakaṃ yajāmahe sugandhiṃ puṣṭi-vardhanam urvārukam iva bandhanān mṛtyor mukṣīya māmṛtāt.*' They washed me with oils and with herbs and dressed me in white – the colour of death. I was taken to the temple where I made my offering of fruits and flowers. Inside the temple, the yogi beckoned me to sit before him, and he chanted '*aum tryambakaṃ yajāmahe sugandhiṃ puṣṭi-vardhanam urvārukam iva bandhanān mṛtyor mukṣīya māmṛtāt*' three times. As he did, he anointed my forehead with powdered ash and spices and flowers of white and yellow and red. He intoned my mantra, '*Aum aim saraswatyai namah,*' and I repeated it three times on my own. He told me that I must repeat this mantra in the morning and in the evening facing the east. He told me that it would bring comfort in times of pain. He said that no longer will I be Sandrine. That Sandrine is no more, that all that she was has been relinquished and forgotten. He gave me the name Sarada, and he told me that I have a purpose. That purpose is to heal. He said that this way I would always focus out and away from my ego and, through this karma yoga, towards my dharma. I accepted my name and my purpose gladly. He said, '*Om Namha Shiva,*' and I was left to repeat my mantra for myself in the temple.

After, I was given a Prasad of almonds and dates, and I was given japa beads. I repeated my mantra on each of the beads, turning them slowly in my fingers.

Saraswati is with me. I know that she always was, but now I feel it with my heart as well as knowing it with my mind. It is a great and powerful comfort, and already she brings me peace and one-ness.

I am home.

Acknowledgements

Writing *Kanyakumari* has been a fascinating and magical journey, one which from the start has been full of strange coincidences and twists of fete, which perhaps I will one day write about. Just like my characters, I didn't know what would happen next and I was happy and intrigued to trust my intuition and let their tales unfold, following them along on their journeys as I travelled through India on successive occasions and *Kanyakumari* began to emerge. I am indebted to the many friends and acquaintances I met along the way who taught me so much about that profoundly captivating country. In particular, I am eternally grateful to Yogi Rama Lingham, to Shane and Lino and Cathy, and to the staff and students of the Sivananda Yoga Vedanta Dhanwantari Ashram. I owe a further debt of gratitude to the many people who have helped me to hone and develop this book post-India. To Maggie, Natalie, the two Johns, Phil, Aaron, Malcolm and the other writers who continued to support and encourage me during the book's development. Certainly there were others who helped in different ways along this novel's path. They know who they are and I remain, as ever, grateful. My heartfelt thanks of course must go to Jan Fortune of Cinnamon Press who believed in this book enough to publish it and who provided such excellent editing and encouragement. Thanks also to Bobbie Darbyshire for meticulous copy editing. Finally, my deepest love, thanks and gratitude to Willow and to Pierre both of whom were there with me on the beach when the sun set to the west of Kanyakumari...

Hazel Manuel, winner of the Cinnamon Press Novel Award, 2013 is a full-time novelist who, following a successful career in business, now lives and writes in Llandudno, North Wales and Paris. When not writing, Hazel is often travelling and her great passion is exploring wild and beautiful parts of the world. Much of her writing is done whilst journeying through off-the-beaten-track places and it wouldn't be unusual to find her in a tent with a notebook after a day trekking in the Sahara or riding a horse across the Andes Mountains. Hazel loves to explore ideas, concepts and places. She acknowledges the influence of writers she reveres, particularly the French Existentialists. "My writing is very much about pushing limits. It is about looking beneath the surface," she says.